T0146688

Sara
and the
Farm

SHARON DEESE

authorHOUSE®

AuthorHouse™
1663 Liberty Drive
Bloomington, IN 47403
www.authorhouse.com
Phone: 1 (800) 839-8640

Published by AuthorHouse   04/06/2017

ISBN: 978-1-5246-8663-5 (sc)
ISBN: 978-1-5246-8661-1 (hc)
ISBN: 978-1-5246-8662-8 (e)

Library of Congress Control Number: 2017905214

Print information available on the last page.

Dedication

This book is dedicated to the one man that I love

with all my heart always and forever.

May God Bless and keep you safe.

Chapter

1

As I sat on the porch watching everyone leave I looked
out over the fields and started thinking on how it all
began. I closed my eyes and it all came to me.

MY NAME IS SARA CROW, I Was born May 19, 1922 to Sam and
Mary Crow. Mom said they were so glad when I was born. They
had two babies that didn't make it before me. We had the old family farm
on 175 acres with a big four bedroom house, three old barns six cows,
twenty sheep, a lot of chickens, plus four pigs. When Grandpa died in
1923 the farm went to dad. He had two brothers and the rest of grandpa's
animals were split between them. Uncle Ray and Uncle Roy were twins
and had their own farms and so they didn't get the farm. My uncles told
dad they would each leave him two cows and a bull. This way he had ten
cows and two bulls and would be able to breed and add to the herd.

Each year at planting or harvest time each of the brothers would help
do each farm. They started with dads, it was spring and the year 1925,
I was three. It had been a long cold winter in Boone County Tennessee.
Our fields were done and the men were working on Uncle Ray's farm. All
the ladies were up at the house working on lunch when Uncle Roy came
running to the house calling mom and Aunt Carol. They took mom over
to the barn and she started crying, Aunt Carol helped her into the house.
Uncle Ray left to get the sheriff and doctor. A team of horses were being
hitched to a wagon and something scared them and they turned and ran,
before they could be stopped they ran over my dad and killed him. Uncle
Roy came back with the sheriff, doctor and pastor. All the kids had to go

into the cow barn and stay there. I was in the house with mom. Soon and big black buggy came, the man talked to my uncles and then he took dad away.

Aunt Kate helped mom fix her black dress, she made me one from Ann's old dress that was too small for her. Two days later we went to church at night. There was a big pine box up at the front of the church. The top was closed and people were going up to it and would put their hands on it and cry or pray. Uncle Roy sat me on his knee and said daddy was in the box waiting for God to come and take him to Heaven. Everyone was saying good-by to dad and praying for a safe trip home with God. He told me that the horses didn't mean to kill daddy and someday God will tell us why, but he must have needed daddy in Heaven to help Him. Then he asked if I wanted to go and say good-by and pray for daddy, yes I did if he would go with me. So he held me and we went up front. I put my hand on daddy's box and told him I loved him and will miss him always, then I asked God to take good care of him. I said good-by daddy and Uncle Ray put me down I ran to mom and didn't know I was crying until she wiped my face. I stayed with her until it was time to leave. Aunt Katy stayed with us that night.

The next morning Uncle Roy picked us up and took us back to church. Uncle Ray's family and a lot of people were there. Pastor had a service and said a lot of nice things about daddy, then we all prayed for him. The bells rang six times then we all stood up, the Pastor led us out the side door to the cemetery. We walked to where the family plot was and there was a big hole. We were told were to sit and then it was quiet, then the bells started to ring again and the men were bringing the pine box to the hole. They started to put daddy in the hole and I started to yell. Uncle Ray picked me up and said God was taking him home not to a hole. God came last night and took your dad to Heaven. Remember how we all prayed and asked Him to take daddy home I said yes, well this is only a place for the box so when you want to talk to him you can come here, but daddy was in Heaven right now so it is ok for the box to go in the hole. Are you ok now? Yes thank you. I was okay the rest of the time. We all went back into the church and we had lunch then Uncle Roy took mom and me home Aunt Katy stayed with us a few days helping mom. Then she went home and was in and out for three weeks. Mom was not feeling well and I was scared she was leaving me too. Daddy died April 19th and I didn't want mom to go too.

One day Aunt Katy was visiting and mom got bad she told me to ring our farm bell till someone came. I started ringing and soon Miss Pepper came running, she went right to mom but told me to keep ringing. Soon Mrs. Anderson and her son Willis came in their buggy. I could stop now, they went for the doctor and my aunts. I was to sit on the swing till they were back. The doctor got there first he went in to see mom, then my aunts came. All I could hear was mom moaning, soon my uncles were there too. I asked Uncle Ray if mom was going to leave me too, all he would say was Sara I don't know. We need to pray so I went to my room and prayed. Just before supper time most were leaving Aunt Kate said I should go home with Uncle Roy, I said no if mom is leaving me I want to be with her here. Aunt Kate made soup and sandwiches for us, my uncles did the chores and said they would send the boys to do them in the morning. Before I went to bed I went to see mom, we talked for a while then said my Prayers. I went upstairs to bed.

The next morning I heard noise downstairs and ran to mom's room. Mom was crying and called me to her. She told me last night God and daddy came and took the baby home with them. He was sick and couldn't stay with us. I told her I didn't know she was having a baby, they didn't tell me in case the same thing happened like before. She was so sorry but it was better this way. We called him Sammy, I asked mom what we were going to do with him and she said we would put his box by dads. That was what we did the next day, just a few friends and family were there. As everyone was leaving I went to dad's cross and told him he had his little boy and mom had me. We would all be fine. Aunt Kate had Ann stay with us for two weeks. She was 15 and out of school, everyone wanted to be sure mom would get better. The day Aunt Kate came to get her mom was crying. She told Aunt Kate she was fine it was just we forgot Sara's birthday. I was called in to the kitchen and Aunt Kate sat me by mom, she told me Sammy died on May 17th and no one remembered my birthday mom and I forgot it too. Sunday we would have a party at Uncle Ray's after church. I was four years old and didn't know it Wow.

It was a great party my aunts and cousins made me clothes, Aunt Carol made me a doll and clothes just like Betty's I loved it. Uncle Roy and Aunt

Carol had three kids, Keith 15, Carl 13 and Betty 10. Uncle Ray and Aunt Kate had five kids, Ann 15, Andy 14, Joan 12, Peter 8 and Mark was 2. Everyone made me a lot of things. Mom and I left around 4 we had chores to do and needed to get home. After chores we made a small dinner then put my stuff away. My toys went into the toy box daddy made me and the clothes in the dresser and closet. We went to sit on the porch and talk. I loved to hear the sounds of the night, and look at the stars. At nine it was time for bed since Sammy went to Heaven mom had me sleep in the small bedroom by her room. She said if she was not in the house when I got up to just sit by the stove till she came in. So in the morning I put on my clothes and waited for her. Starting today we began a new life.

Chapter 2

*T*HINGS DID GET BETTER, MOM and I learned a lot we didn't know there was always one of my uncles there to help us. Now mom's stock was growing and she had to start thinking about what to take to market in a month. They came over to shear the sheep and the Fleece was wrapped we looked over the stock. We were going to take 60 chickens, 30 sheep, 3 calves and 20 pigs. They would be here to help crate the animals. We would go to market one week before harvest started. We still had the new big barn to finish. We needed it before the harvest for the hay, oats, soybeans and corn. We would keep the hay for the animals and some of the oats and corn. The rest mom would sell. Men would come to the farm and look over the crops and make mom an offer for so much of it or all of it. One of my uncles would be there to help mom. The day of the market I stayed with Ann, My aunts went to sell their eggs and would sell moms for her. This was a family affair. Mom came home with a few new animals.

Things were happening a lot this fall. The weather stared getting colder and the harvest would be starting in a week. My uncles were trying to get their crops in. They each had over a 150 acres so they went first. We had to wait for the barn. If not done we will have to use the old one and pray it would keep the crops dry. Sunday after church I went to see dad and told him I knew he was busy with Sammy and I was happy for them, but could he send us a little help with the barn and could he ask God to keep the snow away till the barn was done. Mom and I went to a prayer meeting on Wednesday night and a very nice man came over and talked to mom. He asked her about the barn. She told him what was going on first with my uncles, they would be done we hope in a week or two then do our barn and the harvest. We had the wood and everything needed. Dad and mom used to work on it as much as they could but mom can't do it herself. It is now in God's hands and we pray. He said his name was Mr. Anderson and God sent him to help. Saturday at 6:00, his family and three more families would be there and have a barn raising day there would be nineteen men and boys in all. With God's help it would be done by supper. The ladies would help with the meals. Saturday Mr. Anderson with his wife and six boys, Mr. Brown's family plus two of their uncles made seven men. Mr. Lord were seven men and a boy, and a few of their work hands came to help after their chores. We had over twenty seven men and boys there. God was looking out for us. While the men were setting up the tools the ladies were helping mom with breakfast to get them started. Mrs. Brown was making Oatmeal and rolls. Mrs. Lords was making sausage and gravy and mom was making fried potatoes and scrambled eggs, she made eight loafs of raisin and eight loafs of white bread the day before. We put out her jams and jellies too. We girls put out the tables and set them for the men to eat. When all was ready Mrs. Lords rang the bell. The men washed up and came in the front door to the kitchen picked up a plate, filled it and went to the tables and ate. The ladies filled their cups with coffee and gave them more juice if wanted.

Soon they were back to work and the ladies and girls ate then started on snacks and lunch. Mr. Anderson asked mom to come to the barn with him before they started to see what was to be done. Soon mom was back and you could hear all the noise starting. Mrs. Anderson started two big pots of beef stew. Mrs. Brown was baking in the canning house Mrs. Lords was making kettles of Chicken and dumplings. Mom started her ham and scallop potatoes. We girls made peanut butter and jelly sandwiches for their snack and then some of the ladies and older girls took them to the men around ten with coffee and milk. We could see the trusses and men were soon working on the roof. We all gave up a cheer. At noon Mrs. Anderson rang the bell, they did the same as breakfast, soon all were eating and back to work. Their work hands were now there and more noise was heard. We ate then cleaned up for supper.

At 3:00 mom and Mrs. Brown packed the small wagon with left overs and coffee, milk and water. We started supper. Mrs. Lords and some of the girls were picking apples for pies and apple sauce. Mrs. Anderson and the rest of us girls went to the garden and got more potatoes and stuff for a salad. When we got back mom was frying chicken and peeled potatoes for mashing. Mrs. Lords was cleaning corn. Some girls were helping her while she was making the applesauce. Mrs. Brown was doing cakes and pies, this was the first time mom's kitchen and canning stoves were both going. Mrs. Anderson started the rolls and the gravy. We girls started setting the tables. Some of the older boys made some wood tables and benches so we would all have dinner together. Around 6:00 things started to get quiet Mr. Anderson came and got mom, they went out to the new barn. It was done even painted Red with white trim. The men were washing up and putting their tools and stuff up. Mom came back crying and said it was wonderful and would Mrs. Anderson please ring the bell. We all made our plates and sat down. Mr. Anderson said grace. He thanked God for the nice day and for helping get the work done. For giving each man and boy the strength to work so hard and for the ladies and girls for all their hard work and great food. We all said Amen and ate. After supper the girls helped the ladies clean up their dishes, silverware, pots and leftovers then they went to sit with the men. We kids got to play if not to tired. Then we had cake and pies, coffee and milk. After clean up and packed they were ready to see the barn and go home.

Sunday at church mom got up and thanked God and all the people that did the barn raising on Saturday for us. We had good weather and were ready for our harvest this week. My uncles told them they were so happy that as a thank you they would give each family a half a side of beef this winter. The rest of the harvest went well. As it was done it was put away or sold. Animals were taken to market and we had to think of Thanksgiving. We had a lot to be thankful for this year. With some help from my uncles and their boys we got the work done. I helped with the chores and mom with her baking. It's hard to believe daddy has been gone over six months.

Chapter 3

*S*UNDAY I WENT TO SEE them, told him I missed them and hope they were happy, I know Heaven is a nice place. When I went back into the church mom was talking to the Pastor and a man. He was a worker and was looking for work plus a place to stay. The church would help with his room and board. They would make a room for him in the tool shed next to the barn with a stove, bed and things he would need. Mom said she would talk to my uncles and get back to him. Sunday dinner was at our house so Uncle Roy would let him know on the way home. He would be staying at the pastors for a few days. Nice Sunday dinner, too cold to play outside so the kids all went into the front room and slept or played games. The grownups had their meeting, Uncle Ray's son Keith had a girlfriend and wanted to bring her to Thanksgiving if it was okay with everyone. Then mom talked about the man, there were a lot of questions. She gave Uncle Roy the letter from the Pastor to read. After he read it to the family they all talked. You know Mary, he will be in the house for meals and to bathe, and He would take water out to clean up the rest of the week. All the grown-ups talked it over. Winter was coming and you could see the snow cloud on the way. Mom would be needing more help. Pastor knew this man and said he was a good worker and a fine man. Just on hard times. It would take the church a few days to fix the room, so what did mom think about it? With winter coming she could use the help. I've done the best I could with you and your boys helping mom said. But it would be nice not to be up and out that early in the morning. So my uncles would stop at the Pastors to talk to him they would decide from there. The men left so they could take their time. Pastor would let her know tomorrow. Aunt Carol would drop off Aunt Kate and family at home.

Monday morning Pastor and six men were here at 7:00. Mom went the tool barn with them and decide where to build the room and how big. Dad had a real big tool shed he worked there in the winter so it was build good and warm. The men would build a bedroom, living room and a small toilet room with just a toilet and small sink. Pastor and a man named Frank came into the house with mom. Frank was to live in the room and come into the house for meals and to bathe. Whatever mom needed done he would do. Each morning at Breakfast they could talk over what needed done and she would help where needed. Frank said he would be staying about six months or so. Then going back up north. He would be happy for the work and a place to stay. Then he went out to help with the rooms. Pastor and mom made a list of first morning chores. Frank knew a lot about farming and would be a big help to mom. Holidays and weekends he would go to the Pastors after chores but would be back for evening chores. It took only 1 a day to build the room then they set up the things the ladies sent for him to use. A big bed, sheets, blankets, quilts, couch and two chairs and two lamps with side tables. Since he had a closet he could hang his things. He was all set.

Frank was a nice man but only came to the house to eat and clean up. He worked real hard and mom didn't have to help him much. As Thanksgiving was getting near we had a lot of baking to do, for us and the church families that were on hard times. They would take things home with them after church. Frank went with us to church then to the Pastors for dinner. Pastor would bring him home at night. Mom and I spent the day baking and talking. Next Thursday was Thanksgiving and we had so much to do. After supper we went into our sewing room and worked on our family Christmas gifts. It started to snow just after dark we went out on the porch for a few minutes to thank God for all his help, we would make it through the winter with His help. We went back in and sewed for a while then it was time for bed. We heard Pastor bring Frank home just as I was going to bed. After saying prayers, mom said I would move back up to my room in the spring, was that okay? Yes on my birthday would be fine.

Woke up this morning to a white day. Mom wasn't in the house so I dressed and sat by the table waiting for her. When she came in she told me that one of the cows fall and broke its leg. We had to put her down which means we lost a calf too. Not a good way to start the holiday. Mom sent Uncle Roy the news, he is the one that cuts all the meat for the families. Andy and Peter came along, they were learning to do the job. Mom stored a lot of it but sent some home for the uncle's families. Things would get better soon. Thanksgiving would be here in a few days. Mom started her baking and I got to help with the cookies and the fudge. Thursday it was snowing, not to hard but was not looking good. Frank got the wagon ready and told mom maybe he should take us and drop us off then come back later just in case the weather changed. We stopped to tell the Pastor and leave some things for his family. Then Frank took us to Uncle Roy's house. Families were happy to see Frank was driving, Uncle Roy told him we would be done by 5:00 to come back for coffee. We went in and set the boxes on the table and Frank left.

The kitchen smelled so good. All the kids were playing games in the front room so I was sent there. Keith's girlfriend, Caroline was there and we were making fun till Uncle Roy told us to stop. Soon she was playing games with us. Two O'clock we were called to dinner. Aunt Kate had a very large dining room and we all got to eat at the same time. Everyone over 15 got to sit at the main table, the rest of us at the smaller tables our plates were ready for us. Uncle Ray said Grace and we ate. There was so much that we ate too much and the kids had to take a nap. After the dishes and cleanup was done the adults had a meeting. They listened to Uncle Roy's yearly report it covered all three families. Around 4:30 we were called back for desert and milk. Frank came in as we were eating and said it was getting bad out there and we needed to start for home. As he sat with the men we packed up our stuff.

Soon we were on the road. Pastor and Frank made a place in the back for us to stay warm, it was so nice. When we got home he carried me in and went back to help mom. Next the boxes, put the wagon and horses up then came into the house. He asked mom for coffee and a few sandwiches so he could get evening chores done. He would be up early and would give mom a report at breakfast. I helped mom put the stuff away, ate and then went to bed. I could hear mom in the room she called her office. She was putting things in her book. I got up and ask if things were alright? She smiled and said yes the families had a very good year, and she was adding her share to the book. Uncle Roy already put the money in her bank account. When the weather brakes we will go into town and get things we need for cooking and baking. Plus the things for Christmas, we had lots of gifts to make. I went back to bed and soon I heard her in bed talking to daddy, I closed my eyes and fell asleep.

It snowed all night and Frank came in he said so far so good. All the animals were safe and warm. He would keep an eye on them all day and let her know if he needed her help. He asked for sandwiches and soup he wanted to stay in the tool shed near the pigs and chickens. Sometime that night the snow stopped, no wind and not to cold. After lunch we met Frank in the animal barn. It was nice and warm in there, Pastor and Frank fixed the old wood furnace they had brought here on Thanksgiving. Frank has been setting it up. We always have lots of wood but would only use it when needed. God was looking over us so was daddy. My uncles had heaters in their barns but the wood one would save us electric that was nice.

*C*HURCH ON SUNDAY WAS LOW. There was talk about some men looking at trucks that Ford was selling. My uncles were talking about it at Thanksgiving, sure would be better than a wagon or buggy. Mom said we would have to wait, the tractor was getting old and she would be looking for one soon. Monday we went to town, there was a man there showing off a new truck. Mom and Frank looked at it but not for now. We went shopping and got the things for our gifts. I told mom I was going to make Frank a scarf to help keep his head warm. Most days we baked or worked in the sewing room, things were getting made and wrapped as we went along. Two weeks till Christmas and next Sunday after service we would have a party. The Pastor would hand out a gift to each child to open and the parents of needed families were giving more for their tree. There were also boxes of food for Christmas, most would eat it before so the ladies would make more and on Christmas eve Pastor and some men from church would pick stuff up from the big farms and make more boxes. After 10:30 the stuff would be ready and meat was added the men would take the things to them. Our Church families would all have a great Christmas thanks to all the good people.

After the party Uncle Ray gave us our tree. It was big, he had a lot of them on his farm and gave away a lot each year. Frank put it in the wagon and the ride home smelled wonderful. He would put it in the barn and find the stand. Monday he would bring it into the house. When we got home mom went upstairs for her box of ornaments for the tree. First when we had them all down we unwrapped them, checked to see if the mice got into the boxes and if all were still okay. Some needed to be repaired and some thrown out. Mom showed me the ones she made for me when I was born and the ones she had before she was married. There were some that dad had from his family too. A lot she made and they were so pretty. We will put them near the top of the tree. She said that each year the families would make one for each family to remember them by, only dad's family was doing it. She hasn't heard from her side since they moved to the farm. Mom said as I got older we would put mine in a box so when I got married I would have some for my first tree. Plus I can start making my own too, she would show me how tomorrow and we will put them on the tree. Frank came in for supper and asked when did we want the tree in the house? It sure smelled good in the barn, even the animals liked it. Mom said after lunch would be fine. After supper mom and Frank were talking about the farm and what needed to be done so I went back to the sewing room and my knitting. At four and a half I wasn't too fast but I almost had Franks scarf done. So mom came in and started her knitting, she was making Ann some blue mittens. Ann liked blue.

After lunch Frank hauled in the tree. It was so big that mom asked if he would put the lights on for her. Then she gave him our angel she made and a few ornaments to put there. It was starting to look good. I was so happy we did the rest of the tree, tonight we will turn on the lights for a while. Mom was going to ask Frank if he would like to come in and sit with us by the tree. She was going to make some cider and popcorn. We started dinner, mom made cornbread and beef stew. It was really cold outside and mom was making her bake goods for church. Pastor would be picking them up and taking them to the church for the ladies to pack for the families in need. Mom did pies, breads, cakes, her jams, jellies, green beans and corn that she canned this summer. As she filled the boxes Frank would stack them in the barn. We still had things to do here, everyone was coming here for Christmas, Frank was working in the barn and we were doing the house. Our house was smaller than Uncle Roy's so Frank made two small tables and benches for the kids to sit on, after Christmas he will store them in the barn.

Sunday we packed up the wagon with the frozen meat for the boxes, the sun was out and it was a nice day. Church was full today, all the kids were good. Pastor had a nice service. He told us why we had Christmas and talked about Friday night that Jesus was on his way. He would be born on

Saturday in a manager for all mankind, we need to remember that is the reason for Christmas. After the service we all went downstairs for the party. The kids were sent into one class room to play and the parents to the dining room. At 1:30 we were called into the dining room to eat. After lunch we kids sat on the floor in front of the tree, we sang songs about Christmas then Pastor Louis sat in the big chair by the tree. All was quiet we know what was happening next. One man stood by the tree and Frank on the other side of pastor. Frank would call a name and the child would go to the pastor for a blessing, Pastor would put his hand on your head and ask God to bless and keep you safe. Then the man by the tree would hand you a gift. You were to sit down until all were blessed. This year pastor said on the count of three we could open our gift, we were all shouting till pastor stood up then we stopped. He counted to three and we all tore open our gift, all the girls get new dolls, the boy's trucks. These were store bought toys not homemade like before. My doll had brown hair and a yellow dress. Her shoes were painted on. She was so beautiful. After all was cleaned up we left for home. Pastor would hand out the boxes after all the rest were gone. I heard Frank tell mom that the Elders pulled together and paid for the toys, then the ladies wrapped them. I was asleep when we got home so Frank carried me into my bedroom and mom took off my coat and shoes. When I woke mom was baking again we had to get things going for the church and our families on Friday. Pastor and Frank had everything loaded for fourteen families at the church. Everyone took fresh meat to the church by 7:00pm. Meat was added to the boxes and at 9:00 the men would load their wagons with names and boxes for a few families and go play Santa. Just before bed I set out some cookies and milk for Santa. Mom had to do some chores because Frank was out with the men from church. I was asleep when she came in.

In the morning there were lots of gifts under the tree. I had to wait for the families to get here. Mom had the turkey cooking and the beef roast cooking in the canning house. Frank was watching the one out there. Soon you could smell the turkey. The families started arriving around 1:00. Since it was a nice day the kids could play in the barn or outside. Soon we were called in for dinner. Again there was so much food, after dinner we all went into the front room.

There were so many gifts under the tree. Kids sat on the floor, over all fifteen on chairs or benches. Uncle Ray called out names and Uncle

Roy passed out the gifts. We had to wait till all was handed out. As we opened ours presents everyone liked what they got. After the wrapping was cleaned up the kids played with their toys and the rest of the families sat and talked. At 5:00 we had pie and cake then everyone packed up and started for home. Mom had me take a nap. When Frank came home we would have leftovers for dinner then give Frank his gifts. By 6:30 she woke me to eat. The house was back in order. Frank took the tables and benches to the barn and mom put the rest back in place. After we ate mom put the lights on the tree, to my surprise there were a lot more presents under it. I saw a cradle for my doll and two rocking chairs, one for mom and one for me. Frank made them for us. He loved the things we gave him, mom made socks, two shirts and a pair of gloves. He told me this is the nicest scarf he ever had. He said he made the pastor a big chair for the frontroom, Jane a rocker and James and Joseph each a tool box with some tools in them. So everyone had a nice Christmas and it was time to start thinking about spring and what needed to be done.

The weather wasn't too bad, it snowed off and on not a lot at one time. Uncle Ray said we needed the snow for the crops when we start planting. At church on Sunday Miss Pepper our neighbor said her plow was broken and would someone see if it could be fixed, if not she would need help with the plowing this spring. Frank worked on our tractor and said he would take a look for her. If it couldn't be fixed in time he would plow her fields. Miss Pepper had 40 acres and did all her farm work herself. Soon the weather was getting warm and my uncles and mom went to buy seed. They had decided where they would plant what this year, soon they would be tilling the soil at each farm then go back and start planting. Frank helped my uncles in dad's place they had become good friends. Uncle Roy even said something to mom about him but mom said no. As they went along Miss Pepper's farm was done too. After the ground was ready the seeds were set. Now we just wait and watch. Frank would go to Miss Pepper's ever night after helping my uncles and doing his chores. Miss Pepper's tractor was old and it would take a lot of work. First of March we started having babies, the sheep started lambing, and the pigs had their litters and so many chicks. The cows had to wait till May or June for theirs. Now the work started.

Chapter 5

*F*RANK WENT OUT TO CHECK the fences and make sure it was okay to put the sheep in the field. We had 37 lambs and 79 piglets mom made me stay away from the animals. When they are babies the mom's don't like anyone near them. The sheep and lambs were in the field and we would be tagging the piglets today. Frank, my uncles and their boys were all here early. First they had to separate the mom from the babies. They put a tall long board across the bottom of the gate then would put apples and slop in a feeding box and then open the gate so the mom would get over the board and the gate was shut. As she ate the guys would get one or two at a time and put mom's tag on its ear. When done mom was let back in and the board was moved to the next stall. With only three sows it didn't take long then on to my uncles farms. They had more sows so it took most of the day. Frank was back in time for chores and mom helped him. Then he would go to Miss Pepper's, she had less animals than we did. She had nine cows, one bull, ten sheep and two pigs. She had two ducks and two turkeys, she was going to let them lay and hatch some eggs and take them to market. Mom told her that she can breed her sheep and pigs with our studs if she wanted to increase her stock. That would be wonderful. One Sunday after church we saw Frank taking Miss Pepper to the pastors for dinner. Pretty soon he told mom he was going to have dinner over there once in a while.

By the middle of April we started shearing the sheep, ours first then my uncles. In the late afternoon Frank would do his chores then go to Miss Pepper's. The pastor's sons would come and help with the animals. Easter was next week and there was a lot to do. Mom was taking 30 lambs and 70 pigs to market, plus 60 chickens and 40 dozen eggs. Mom went with

Frank, my uncles and their boys. For Easter we would have dinner at Uncle Roy's house. Mom made a ham and rolls, she made two pies too. Before dinner we had an Easter egg hunt. The older kids helped us younger ones. It was lots of fun, the one with the most eggs won a half dollar. We had lots of food the boys are getting bigger and eating a lot more than before. We had cake and pie then cleaned up and started for home. In the morning at breakfast mom asked Frank if he knew when he was going to head up north, he put a big smile on and said he asked Emma to marry him and she said yes. The wedding would be the 29th of June when her brother could get here. We were so happy for them. Please tell her we will be happy to help her with the wedding. Frank said her name was Emma and he would tell her. Mom said she would like to have them to dinner on Friday night if they would like, he will check. Plus Sara we have to plan your birthday you will be five this year and start school this fall. Frank went back to work. We will have to make something nice for their wedding so we need to go to the store and see what is new. Mom decided we were going to make a table cloth and eight napkins. As we passed her farm you could see all the pretty flowers she planted so mom had a plan. At the store we looked at all the patterns till we found just the right one. Then mom bought yards and yards of white linen. Soon we were looking at the threads so many colors. Now we were all set. At night we would go into the dining room and she would have the linen laid out on the table. First she cut the table cloth then the napkins. She hemmed everything then she pressed the patterns on. Next we matched the colors with the flowers and leafs. The table cloth was first than the napkins. Mom then wrote down all the colors to what flowers and the numbers, there were a lot of colors. Some flowers had two colors and some had three. Mom would do the table cloth and me the napkins. My cross stitching was getting pretty good. So after dinner we sat in the sewing room and worked on them.

Before long mom said we had to get started planning my birthday party. She said it would be better to have it on a Saturday so the kids could play outside and not in their church clothes. We sent a note to my uncles and mom asked Frank and Emma to come. We would have fried chicken, potatoes salad, beans, corn on the cob and cake and ice cream. It was set for 3:00 but everyone was there by 2:30 to help mom. The kids played games and in the barn, my uncles helped Frank in the barn and talked about what was going to happen when he got married. They told him he sure did a great job and would be missed. The ladies called all of us to eat at 4:30 and by 5:30 I was opening my presents. I had 6 new dresses for school, a pair of shoes, a nice gray sweater from Aunt Kate and toys from the others. Frank and Emma gave me a tablet and pencils so I could learn to write. Crayons and paper to draw things on. I was a happy little girl. Next we had cake and ice cream so everyone could head for home. We had church in the morning.

That night mom and Frank spent a lot of time upstairs and Emma helped me learn to write my name. Soon it was quiet and they came down stairs. Mom made coffee and we had more cake, I had milk. We talked about the wedding. It was only six weeks away. My uncles and their families were helping with the food and church all mom and Emma had to do is our dresses and flowers. Frank left to take Emma home and we had to put my things away. I took my box of toys and stuff up the stairs right behind mom. At the top she turned right, my room was left so I stopped. Mom said to follow her. Frank and mom moved all my things into a new room. I don't know when they had time. It was painted, and mom made a quilt and curtains it was so beautiful all I could do is walk around and just look. Mom hung up my dresses and just watched me. I asked how she did all this and she said when we would go into town Frank took all the things to the tool shed. Then he and the pastor's sons painted and put down the rugs. As he fixed and painted the hutch and desk he would return them when we were gone. He even made me a hope chest and cleaned up my toy box that daddy made me. Mom said he picked up my bed and dresser when he went to town. She had the stuff for the quilt and curtains at Christmas and worked on them when I was sleeping or napping. I was now five and ready for a big girls room. On the wall I had a cross and a picture of daddy. Mom said while we were playing my aunts helped clean out the room down stairs and all my things were in the dresser. I took out a nightgown and got ready for bed. We said our prayers and mom said she would leave my door open some so if I needed her all I had to do is call. She turned off the light and said I love you Sara, and told her I love you too then she went down stairs. The moon put a nice warm touch in the room, I knew I would be fine. In the morning I gave Frank a kiss and big hug for my room and all he did. He just smiled and said you're welcome.

Chapter 6

AFTER CHURCH WE WORKED WITH the chickens. Counting and seeing how many would go to market in the second week of June. Every two months we send chickens and eggs to market it helps pay the bills. This time I get to go too. The chickens that were going to market were put in a new pen, mom and I started to feed them and the four hogs we were taking. The cows were starting to calf, one cow had twin girls small but doing fine. The other had a boy he cried a lot and ate like a pig. The lambs we kept were bigger now and we had twenty to go to market. Maybe we will find a cow or two if the price is right and Frank and uncles say okay. It is getting warm. Emma and mom are working on planning the wedding. We will have the reception in the church fellowship hall, my aunts have all the food planed and some ladies from the church are helping and making baked goods for them. Mrs. Anderson makes wedding cakes so she is helping too. So mom and Emma started working on the dress and veil, she would have flowers from her gardens in church and for her and mom to carry.

On Saturday Emma and Frank went into town and came back with a big bed and two dressers. Emma had been sleeping in the room she had since she was six and had a small bed. The big bedroom was empty when her dad passed away her brother John took all the bedroom stuff to his home. Now they had a new room to make up. The ladies at church had a sewing day for her, it was like a shower. She had all the things for the house. Just needed things for the new bedroom. So they made sheets and pillow cases, quilts and doilies. Curtains to match the wedding quilt and rag rugs for the floor. New bathroom towels and as the things were done the younger girls would iron them and pack them to go to Emma's house. When we were done I never saw so many things, we had dollies, table cloths and napkin sets, three lap robes, towels, wash cloths, pot holders made by the little kids, aprons and dish cloths. So many boxes. Each family gave some jars of vegetables, fruit, jellies and jams. One more week till the wedding. After we packed the wagon mom told Emma since it was late we would come over in the morning and help her unpack. Emma said great because she was tired too. We went home and to bed I was tired and so was mom.

On a bright June morning one week till the wedding after frank went to do chores we left for Emma's. Mom helped unpack a lot of the things for the bedroom, they made the bed and hung the curtains, put out the dresser scarfs and laid the rag rugs on each side of the bed. The room looked very nice. Then she showed me her wedding dress, it was a light blue and had lace on it from her mother's wedding dress. She was going to be a lovely bride. Mom's dress was a darker blue and she would wear a hat. They will carry flowers from Emma's garden. Uncle Roy was to pick us up and take us to the church. Frank had their wagon and left our place early, the big day was here, Frank dropped us off at Emma's and went to the pastor's. Emma and mom went to the garden and cut flowers. Then they took them to the barn and cut and shaped them and put ribbon to match the dresses on them. We had one hour before Uncle Roy would be here. I got to wear a new school dress, it was yellow with small white flowers on it. Mom got ready then helped Emma. Uncle Roy was right on time, we put our things in his buggy. He was going to bring us home to night. When we got to the church Uncle Roy went to the back so we could go into the basement. There we met Emma's brother, he was a small skinny man and didn't have much hair he didn't look happy till he saw Emma. He put on a great big smile and started to cry. He gave her a big hug then they went to a table to talk. His name was John and he was twenty years older than Emma. He lost his wife and his kids were grown and moved away from where he lived. So he was all alone. Soon the pastor came down and ask if she was ready, yes she said. He said a prayer for all there and asked God to bless this marriage. I went up and sat with the families.

The music started and Pastor, Frank and James came out the side door and walked to the front. Now it was quiet the music started again and the doors at the back opened and mom came down the aisle to the front. This time we stood up as the music started, the doors opened and Emma and John came into the church. She was a ray of sunshine and John had a big smile on his face. Emma took a flower and put it in a small hole on John's coat. As they came to the front I looked at frank he had a tear in his eyes and a large smile on his face. Pastor did a fine service and when they kissed everyone clapped. Then pastor said he was happy to present Mr. and Mrs. Frank Lawrence. Then Frank and Emma walked to the back and mom and James were next. Pastor and John went next then the rest of church followed to the basement. The ladies had the food ready and we ate. There was a man and woman there, the man played the piano and the lady sang. Everyone was talking to Frank and Emma, John sat with us and was having a good time with my uncles. He went to school with them and they were going over old times and laughing a lot. Some people were dancing and having a good time. By 6:00 Uncle Ray had all the meat ready for anyone that wanted some to take. As Frank and Emma left, we threw rice at them. Mom said they were going to a hotel in town for the night. It was a small honeymoon. John was staying there too. So Uncle Ray said he would drop him off. Uncle Roy took us home and we had a quiet night.

Mr. Anderson's sons did our chores but mom and I would be back at it in the morning. After morning chores we went to church, everyone was still talking about the wedding. When we got home Frank was there getting his things. He and mom had a talk, if she could feed the stock in the morning he would be over after breakfast to cleanup and do all the heavy stuff till she could fine new help. She is hopping to fine someone the first week of August at the market. She was also going to look for two cows. He was going to go along and help my uncles. Frank pulled the wagon hauler with the chickens, pigs and sheep in it. Emma, mom and I were in the buggy with 45 dozen eggs. We met my uncles at the church and on to market. As we pulled up to the pens we were told where to put the animals. My aunts took mom's eggs with them and we stayed with mom for a while. She has to watch her stock. Men would come by and look then move on to the next pen. A few men came back to make an offer for some or all the sheep or pigs she would think about it and they would haggle over the price. Mom was pretty good at this and my uncles were proud of her. Uncle Roy said he would watch the stock and Uncle Ray would take her to see the cows that were for sale and check the office for men for hire. People were coming and going all over the place. Emma and I went to look at the market tents. They had some nice things but mom said I had to have someone with me if I found something I liked. I got some candy and ribbons for my hair. Then we went back by the stock. Uncle Roy sold the rest of mom's stock and Aunt Carol gave mom the money from the eggs. Mom and Uncle Ray came back with three cows, two heifers and a bull. They didn't look like the ones we had. Uncle Ray said they were good strong cows and he wants to take them to his farm for breeding maybe we can improve our herds. With the stock sold and eggs done mom said she still had some money left over after paying for the cows. Then we went to see if there was any good help left. There was a list and paper work on each person they were all checked out with the police too. There was one that stood out to all of them only one thing, he had a wife. They said you don't pay for her she is what you call a plus. She will help around the farm and do what you say. So we talked to them, told them what mom would pay and what she wanted done. Frank told them about the room and that there was a large bed in it. It was warm in the winter and cool in the summer. He told them we would be back in an hour to see if they wanted the job or not.

We went looking around the market and mom found a few things she needed. A new pot for her jellies and jams, some cloth and thread, yarn and soaps. When we got back they said it was a fine offer and they would be glad to take it. They had an old buggy and horse and would follow us home if it was alright. Uncle Ray loaded the three black cows and Frank took our hauler, mom took our buggy and we all started out. Frank would pick up Emma at our farm after he showed the Evans around. Emma, mom and I started dinner. Mom had a list that Frank helped her make out, it was the work that needed to be done. She had to let them know that Frank and my uncles would help when needed. When Frank finished the tour they came into the house and we showed the wash sink, kitchen and bathroom. If they need more ask mom. We sat down to eat, the man's name was George and his wife was Jenny, he was 28 and she was 26. After dinned Frank helped George with the chores and Jenny helped with the kitchen. She asked mom if we went to church, mom said yes did they want to go too. Yes if they could, mom told her they could take baths on Saturday and use hot water in their room the rest of the week. This made her happy so she left for their room to unpack. In two weeks we will start the harvest so things will start getting busy, we will see then how things go. Emma and Frank left soon after chores. Frank had things to do at home.

UNDAY MORNING GEORGE AND JENNY followed us to church. They met the pastor, his family and a few more people then they went to town. Everyone was talking about the phone company, they been putting lines in our area. There is to be a meeting at church on Tuesday night at 7:00. No kids so Mrs. Brown is going to drop off Carrie to stay with me. Last week we saw men putting tall poles in down our road. We knew something was happening. In two weeks right after Labor Day school will start. Next week mom and I will walk to school and put my name in the book and she can fill out the papers, then I will be set to go. In the morning mom and I still feed the chickens and pigs, George did the cows and sheep. Uncle Ray brought back the three cows and we started to have so much milk for the milk company. They were coming twice a week to pick it up but now it was three times. Uncle Ray is bringing over the milking machine and Uncle Roy will help set them up. Tuesday mom went with Mrs. Brown and Carrie and I worked on our sewing. We talked about school. She would be going into town for school this year, so would Joey. She was in tenth grade and Joey was in ninth. Our school only had Kindergarten to eight grade. At 8:30 I went to bed, didn't know when mom came home I would see her in the morning. She was telling George and Jenny we would be getting our phone in two weeks. There are nine farms on our road and we would be on a party line. We were number seven on the line. When the phone is put in that will give us a number. If we wanted to make a call you would pick up the phone and someone would ask what number you wanted. It would be better than ringing the bell.

Friday mom and I started for school, it was at the end of the road. As we passed the six farms mom told me their names and that if it started to rain or something was wrong to go to one of the houses and they would call her. I met my teacher, her name is Miss Miller. She had all eight grades in one room. She showed me where my desk was and then talked to mom. There was a piece of paper on my desk with my name on it. I just sat at my desk and looked at it. Miss Miller said first day of school I was to bring paper, pencils and crayons to school also my lunch. We walked back home. Mom said it would take an hour to walk to and from school. Soon the harvest would start and she would be busy and couldn't take me. I told her I would be fine. There were some of the Anderson kids still going to my school and I would walk with them. Sunday at church mom talked to Mr. Anderson about me walking with the boys. He told her that Matt was thirteen and would be taking the buggy so it was no trouble. Mom said she would be glad to pay if he would, so Mr. Anderson called Matt over. Mom told him what she needed and she would pay him 50 cents a week. Yes, he would be glad to do it have her ready be 8:30. He would let mom know if he had to go in early to clean the blackboards.

Early Monday morning I heard the tractors coming up the road. Emma came to help mom and the ladies with the food. Emma told mom that Frank did their farm over the week end so he could help my uncles. After chores George went to help in the fields and Jenny helped in the house. Around 9:00 the phone company showed up. A man asked where she wanted her phone. She told him on the wall in the kitchen. Where was the other one to go? In the sewing room on the table. It took about an hour and then he checked the line, our number was to be 8025m1 we were to give it to the people that we wanted to have it. When my uncles came in for lunch they gave mom their numbers and took ours. Emma said it was easy to remember hers was 8025r1. The man had the office call mom so she would know what her ring sounded like, it was 2 long and 2 short rings. We were on a party line and all the farms had a different ring. By supper time the fields were done and put up, we would start to bag the soy beans next week after they dried. They will start at my uncles tomorrow, it will take two weeks.

School started today and Matt and the boys picked me up. Matt had me sit up front with him. He would help me in and out of the buggy. The first day he made sure I found my seat. Miss Miller was a nice lady and good teacher. She had all of kindergarten and first grade write down our names and numbers as far as we could go then our ABC if we knew them. With Emma's help I could write to 50 and all my ABC's big and small. That was fun, then we had recess and were able to play under the trees. The older kids played ball and we played on the swings. After recess we were giving books so we could start reading. The book was called Dick and Jane. It was nice I liked the pictures. Not sure of all the words. After school Miss Miller ask me how I learned all the things I could write. I told her Mrs. Lawrence showed me. She asked me to see if she would call the school and gave me a note for her. As soon as I got home I gave mom the note, she called Emma and read it to her. Emma would go and see Miss Miller tomorrow at lunch time. Since it was nice out we ate our lunch under the trees. I met two girls from my class they didn't live on my road but we became friends. Miss Emma and Miss Miller had a long talk. Then Emma went home. I was glad I wasn't in trouble and tried to be good the rest of the day. Matt had to clean boards today so we were late getting home. Mom said George had to take Jenny to see the doctor so we were having dinner at Emma's. It was a nice walk and mom asked me all about school. Before I knew it we were there. Emma had dinner ready and as we ate she asked me about school, if I liked it and did I learn anything yet. I told her it was fine and fun. We are trying to learn to read Dick and Jane. She told us that Miss Miller asked her if she would like to teach K-3 a few days a week. Would I be okay with that? Yes that's fine. Frank said the extra money would help. She was to talk to the school board at the meeting on Friday night. They were happy to have someone to help and she would start on Monday. She would have kindergarden-3rd grade. There were 6 kids in my grade, 9 in first grade, 2 in second and 4 in third. That sure helped Miss Miller out.

George and Jenny were back and wanted to talk to mom. I got ready for bed. In the morning mom said Jenny was sick and they would have to go back home to Georges family. His dad and brothers were adding a room for them and hopped to have it ready in two weeks. Ohio was getting cold already and snowing so it would be slow going. Jenny had to see the doctor every two weeks. She had to take it easy. Mom and I made some warm things for them to take to Ohio it was very cold there. I would ask dad after church to watch over them. George was still working hard and mom was looking for new help to start in January. It started to get cold so mom made me a quilt to keep me warm. Matt made sure I stayed warm and dry when it rained. The holidays came and went soon the first of the year was here. George's dad called the men from his church to come and help with the room and it was done. Ladies from church made sheets and quilts for the bed. All was ready for them to come up. Everyone from church helped with warm clothes and food from the train ride there. The church paid for their tickets and the doctor gave her meds and the name of a doctor to see as soon as she could. Frank took them to the train station in his new truck. Bill came back with him.

Chapter 8

FRANK SHOWED BILL ALL THE things that needed to be done every day, chores he had in the morning and evening and where to clean up and eat. I didn't really like him, I don't think mom did either but we needed the help and Frank and my uncles were always there to help if we needed them. It started to snow on Friday night. We had a foot of snow in the morning and it was cold. Bill came in that evening and said all was well with the animals. Mom gave him some extra soup to take to his room. All week-end it snowed off and on. Miss Miller called Sunday night and said there would be no school until she called again. It snowed four more days. The farmers tried to keep their driveways and our part of the road clean, Frank had to come and tell Bill what to do. I was so glad when Frank and Emma came over for lunch the next day. I asked Frank if I could talk with him. I told him that Bill had been drinking and not doing some of the things mom said had to be done. He would check on it. Emma said school would start the next day to be sure I wear long pants under my dress. By the end of February most of the snow was gone. We started to work on what animals would go to market and mom started with the chickens and eggs. Frank came over to make the egg crates because Bill forgot to do them. He didn't put the sheep that had lambs in the pens either. My uncles and families came for Sunday dinner and to start planning the market and the new planting season. As we ate my uncles asked Bill about the animals and what was ready for market. He didn't know anything so after dinner Frank and my uncles and the boys went out to check everything. When they came back in they gave mom her report. She had 63 lambs even 3 black ones. 103 baby chicks and 91 chickens. What did she want done? She would sell 60 lambs keep the black ones, 100 chicks, and 40 chickens. She had so many eggs that the egg man can't keep up. After Bill went back to his room my uncles told mom he was not doing his job and they found whisky bottles all over the place. When we go to the market we will look for a new man.

Market day was tomorrow so mom took her cookie jar down and counted the money she was saving for her truck. This was her special money and there was $1103.00 all she needed was $800.00 more and we would get it. Mom didn't buy things on time only cash. Bill said the drivers would be here in the morning to pen up the lambs and the milk company just left. My uncles came over to have a talk with Bill, they told him he wasn't needed any more. He could go to the market and see if there was more work or leave today so we can bring home someone else. He was going to go to town and take the train up north. He had a sister in New York and he would go there, sorry things didn't work out. Frank came over that night to crate the chickens. Mom told him that Emma was picking us up at 6:30 and that we would be back by 5:00 to do chores. Mom made a roast for dinner and packed a lunch for Bill for on the train. She even gave him an extra $20.00 dollars in his pay. Emma was there at 6:30 sharp and we were off. It was a busy day, mom's chickens went fast so did her eggs. The lambs stock started at noon so mom went with the men and Emma and I sold all Emma's eggs. She said it was nice having a man around the house. Since all the eggs were gone we walked around the market. I had my spending money from my chores so I got more paper and crayons, some yarn and cloth and patterns. Mom's number was called and we went to watch. Mom sold 40 lambs to one man and the rest to the second man. She was very happy she told my uncles, with the lambs, chickens and chicks plus the eggs she made $ 1400.00. They told her to get to the bank first thing in the morning to deposit the checks. Then we went to the office looking for a new helper. There was a man about fifty, he use to have a farm but left it when his wife died. He looked like a good hard working man and could answer all the questions my uncles and Frank asked. So Walter came to work for us and I liked him right away. He rode home with Frank so they could talk. When we got home Frank and Walter went to do chores. We went to start dinner. As we went into the kitchen mom stopped, she told Emma to get Frank.

Bill took mom's money from the cookie jar and took her horse. In Tennessee horse stealing was a hanging crime. Frank called the sheriff, mom told the police she had $1103.00 in the jar. She was going to get her truck next week. Sheriff told mom he had a twelve hour start but he had radios that work faster we just have to wait. My uncles got there as the police were leaving. Uncle Ray told her he would take her to the bank and help he open a savings account so she could keep the money separate. Frank helped Walter move into his room, he said this is the best place he worked in a long time. Then they came in to eat. It was late when we got to bed and we had church tomorrow. I had a lot to tell dad. We asked Walter if he wanted to go to church with us he said not this week. I went and talked to dad, told him how well mom was doing till now. I told him about the market and Walter. Next week I will bring new flowers for their graves, it was Easter and I wanted them to look nice. Told him I bet God would be happy to have His son back home. When we got home Walter was talking to the police, they came over to mom and told her they found Bill. The horse died from being ridden so hard and it was old. Bill was in a bar and telling the story about the horse and money so the bartender called the sheriff and they picked him up he still had $947.00 on him and he will be back in town by Saturday. This made mom feel better. She called my uncles and they told her she may have to go to court, we will have to wait and see. The sheriff came to the house on Saturday and gave mom her money. They were going to charge him with horse theft, mom will only have to sign some papers and he will be turned over to county and they will charge him. She will be in the clear and nothing will come back on her. Our name won't even be mentioned and that was good. Uncle Ray took mom to the bank and opened a saving account for her. She put the check for $ 947.00 and $231.00 cash in it. As soon as she has $1500.00 in it she will look for a truck.

Walter told mom he got a letter from his son and can't read all of it would she help him, sure bring it in at dinner and she will help. The day was going fine school was soon going to be out for the summer, I was doing well in school. I was bringing home all my papers and had stars and numbers on them. I was having a little trouble with my spelling but so was the rest of the class. After dinner we sat and read Walters letter. His son James wrote Dad. We have to decide what to do with the farm. The people that were leasing are moving on and we need you here to tell us what to do. Are we going to try and lease it again or sell it, you know it has been in the family for 127 years and it is still in your name, please tell us what to do. Lease it or sell it, I can lease it but you have to be here to sell it. Plus there is a lot of money in the bank in your name from the leasing. Can you call me so we can talk or send me a number and I will call you? The Swan's will be moving in two months. Your son James. Mom told him he could use our phone to call him or for him to call here just let her know. He said he would think about it and tell her what he was going to do after the first of May. We didn't have a family dinner for Easter most of the kids were sick and so everyone stayed home. Frank and Emma went to the Pastor's and Walter had dinner here. Ham, sweet potatoes, corn rolls, applesauce and apple pie. Walter said that was the best meal he had since his wife died. Mom asked if he wanted to talk about her, yes that would be nice.

Her name was Alice and she was a good wife and mother. They had four kids and the doctor said not to have any more. Her health was poorly. There was something wrong with her heart and no one knew how to fix it. She was to take it easy. Things were fine for four years, the kids did the house work and chores. She had planned the whole week for house chores, who would do what and when. If not in the house then you worked with dad. One day when the kids were in school she decided that the clothes needed to be done, she brought them all to the cellar and washed them. Then out to the lines to hang them. When the kids got home they found her on the ground dead. The doctor said it was a heart attack she was only forty nine. That was five years ago. I left the farm after we laid her to rest. We were married for thirty years, when I lost my wife I lost my life. The kids took over the house I told them to do as they would. I didn't care. Now I have to do what is right I'm going there in two months and have a meeting with the kids, if one of them want it I will give it to them. If not we will sale it and I will give them each a share of the money. So I'm sorry I will only be here for six weeks then go to stay with James. I hope you will be able to find someone to help you by then.

Chapter 9

*A*T CHURCH MR. ANDERSON TOLD mom that he had two boys looking for work, and if she would take them on it would be wonderful. They had to start earning money if they wanted to build their home and start thinking of getting married. Mom talked to them and agreed on a pay. They would start soon. Walter worked with them for a week then he left. The boys moved in. They brought two small beds so each had their own. Monday was a day off school and since it was raining we sat in the sewing room working on our quilts. Mom was making one for the fair in July. I was using the scrapes for a baby quilt. Soon I was tired and went to bed. In the morning it was still raining and the boys were wet when they came in. Mom told them to go change clothes and that there were wind breakers in the tool shed to get them and come back. Mom made eggs, bacon and pancakes for us, and lots of coffee. They were happy for the wind breakers. Mom told them to always ask if they didn't have something. They talked about the pigs getting ready to birth and the cows calving soon and how was she at helping with all of that, she told them just to call her. Market was again at the end of June so we would have a lot to take with us.

The third week of May was the last week of school. All week we had fun we had picnics and play day, then we had to clean out our desks and wash them down. The last day of school Miss Miller said she was getting married that summer, but would be back to teach in September. The 19th of May was my birthday and I had a party at my house with family and friends. I was now six years old. I received a lot of nice things. The 20th was the last day of school. We took our name tags off our desks. We could take them home if we wanted. This was my first one so it went home with me. It was hard saying goodbye to my friends for the summer, you don't know who will move or be back next fall. Then the teachers stood by the door and called our names. They would give us a hug and wish us a safe and fun summer then give us our report cards so we could leave. If you had a red star you passed, all my grades had red stars but one that was spelling it was blue. But most were red so I passed. I was now in 1st grade and as happy as could be.

Two more weeks and off to the market again. Ninety-nine pigs were going and all were tagged. Six calves going to market were tagged, sixty chickens and forty dozen eggs. We would still have a week if we decided on more. Mom said to add twenty chickens. So that made eighty, and add two more calves. Two cows still didn't have their calves so she would still have some all the bulls but two went. Mom left food for the boys they were staying and doing chores she packed lunch for all of us. Emma and my aunts would bring food too. Trucks started coming at 5:00 and Emma was there at 6:30 we were off. As we rode to the market Emma would giggle every once in a while. Finely mom asked her what was going on, she pulled off the road and said we are going to have a baby. Everyone was laughing and crying we were so happy for them. She pulled back on the road and we talked about the baby. It would be here in November around Thanksgiving. She told mom she went to see the doctor a week ago he said both were doing fine. Frank was on cloud nine, but wanted to wait till today to tell anyone. So now we were talking babies all the way to the market. I asked if she was still going to teach this year. She said yes till November when the doctor told her to stay home. The school knew about it and was looking for a sub to cover her till she could come back. Mom went off with the men and I stayed with Emma till all the eggs were sold. A man left his card and asked if we would give it to mom, and one for Emma. At noon we all had lunch by the trucks. Mom asked Frank if next week when there was time would he help her find a truck. Sure thing just name a date. We then went to watch the pigs sell. All of ours went, then the calves' mom sold all eight and all the chickens. Mom and my uncles went looking for horses but didn't find any good ones so they would wait till next time. But they came back with a really nice brown pony, it was mom's late birthday present for me. It was time I learned to ride. Wow

Emma is having a baby and I get a pony what a day. Frank was bringing it home for me. I had to name her, I asked mom how you name a pony. You have to watch her and see how she acts you need to talk to her and then a name will come to you. I was going to give it a try. When we got home the boys had a stall ready for her. Mom told them last week she was going to look for one for me. They put a short gate on it so I could feed her and sit and talk to her, she had her own yard and I could see her there. I had a blanket and saddle for her, she was broken and ready to ride. She was feeling right at home. She found her food and water so she would be fine for the night. I told her good night and went in for supper. This was going to be a fine summer.

Frank and mom found her a nice truck, and he was teaching me to ride my pony. I was learning fast. I had been on horses with my dad a lot but not since he died. I knew how to saddle a horse so a pony was easier. I talked to her all the time still no name, here it was July and I started writing down names and when she was in her yard I would call her one to see if she would come to me, as she was eating I would call her a name and wait to see if she would come to me. She didn't like names in A-B- C or D lists but I was sure we would have one soon, I could feel it. She was getting fat and hard to put the saddle on her so mom called the vet. After he checked her out he said not to ride her any more she was going to have a baby, in two months. No one knew she was pregnant so this was a great deal for mom. After everyone left I started talking to her and said Honey Girl you're going to be a mommy, with that she picked up her head and came to the gate. I looked into her eyes and I knew her name was Honey Girl. After that any time I would call Honey she would come right to me. Everyone was happy she had a name. So in September Honey was to have her baby and November Emma. I made a nice warm blanket for the colt and a quilt for the baby. Mom and I stared on baby clothes and I learned to make gowns, bunting and a crib blanket. My cross stitching was very good so I put patterns on them too. I had three towels with ducks and three wash cloths. As I finished I would put them in a box in my room.

Church was slow, people were on vacation but we had a new family move in to the house on Mr. Brown's farm. He had two boys, one was nine months old and the other was three. Pastor said the mom was lost when the baby was born. They moved here to start a new life. Mr. Larson had a job lined up but needed a sitter for the boys so he could start work. After church pastor asked mom if she would help him out, even till he could find someone else mom said sure she was going to watch Emma's when she went back to work. Mr. Larson would pay her $25.00 a week, he worked from eight till five. He would bring the boys at 7:30 and pick them up around 5:30. On the week-ends he would help around the farm. Mr. Anderson two sons were still working here and that would help pay them. Lee and Stu did all the farm work so mom had only the house and her garden. We fixed the small room down stairs into a nap room for the boys. Mom had a crib for the baby but would need a sheet or two till she could make some more. There was the small bed I used that the three year old could use. We were ready for them. Wednesday Mr. Larson came over to set up the small bed and for the boys to meet mom and me. Peter was three and Paul was nine months they took to mom right away. They put a gate up by the stairs so the boys would be safe. They would start coming on Monday so mom said they should come to dinner after church it would help them get used to us. Monday after their dad left they cried a little but mom had food ready and they loved to eat. Aunt Betty gave mom a high chair for Paul to use this way he could feed himself. The only time the little ones saw the boys was at lunch and dinner. Lee and Stu knew how to handle little ones so it was fine. Soon the boys had new toys that Lee and Stu made for them to play with. Peter loved his stick pony and would play all the time in the house or side yard where the boys put up a fence for them.

Chapter

10

SINCE WE ATE AT 6:00 Mr. Larson would stay and eat with us. Then he would take the boys home, sometimes Paul cried. This gave dad time to play with the boys before bed. It was working out fine, mom and I still had our time in our sewing room. We got to know him and him us. His name was Larry and he was twenty eight, two years older than mom. His wife Sally passed away two days after Paul was born and her family wanted the boys. He said no he would handle things his way. So for the next eight months someone from her family was always there. So he came to our town looking for a house and job. As soon as he found one he left Wisconsin and moved here. It was a long trip and he only had a two bedroom house so no one could come and stay. He was happy now, things would get better. On the week-ends they would come over and help with the gardens. One day he asked mom if she would go with him to the church dance they have once a month. It was for singles only. She said she didn't know there had to be someone to watch the kids, someone they knew. Lee looked up from dinner and said they know us we would be happy to do it. Mom looked at me and I told her to go she needed to have some fun. It was from 7:00- till 10:00. It had been three years since dad died and he wouldn't want her to sit home all the time. It was time so she said yes. Larry was very happy too. So he picked her up at 6:45 and said she would be home by 10:15 if that was okay with me, sure I will be in bed sleeping. She looked so pretty I was glad to see them going to have a good time. The boys were staying the night. School would start soon so I went back to do my writing and spelling. Plus we had market the end of August. We counted the pigs, chickens, ducks and two calves. Frank and the boys went along and since mom and Emma were selling now to the egg man we didn't have eggs to sell so our day was free. Emma went to sit with Frank and we went to mom. Uncle Ray told mom she was doing a great job and didn't need their help anymore. If she need help just yell and one of them would come over. They asked her about hers and Larry's friendship and if anything was going on. She wasn't sure yet but would like Larry and the boys to come to Thanksgiving since it was at her house. Everyone said sure they all liked him too.

We were going to ride a school bus this year. Mom had to call and see what time I had to be ready. The bus would go passed us going to the Andersons first then me so I had to listen for it and be ready. I would see it coming back down the hill and go to the mail box, wait for it to stop, then cross over and get on. The bus stopped and picked up Emma then the rest of the kids. By now the boys were calling my mom ma or mom. She wanted to know if I was upset, maybe a little I just didn't know, why. She said I call her mom all the time so they were doing what I did. They are so young and did what an older kid would do. She would try and have them call her Miss Mary if it made me happy. No it was fine and if they were going to follow me I better watch what I do and say. It was like being a big sister. Labor Day was Monday and school started on Wednesday the first day for the bus. All my new dresses were ready, I grew two inches this summer and would have to try and make them a little longer mom will get it done. As I got on the bus I met the driver, his name was Mr. Owens. He told us where to sit, next was Emma she sat with me. It was by grade so I sat in front. When we stopped at school he told us where the bus would be after school he would be waiting for us there. When we get to the class room on the black board it had the teacher's names. Miss Miller was now Mrs. Walker and she would be doing 4-8 grades and Mrs. Lawrence had K-3 our names are on the desks so please take your seat. Our books were on our desks. We had to put covers on all of them to keep them in good condition. Mrs. Lawrence told us to work on our covers then take our spellers and start writing our list we had to learn. We would be having a test on Friday. The only noise was the paper moving. Mrs. Walker was working with her group with their reading. The day went fast soon it was time to go home. We had to take our spelling home for homework. We had to write each word 10 times and read the first story in our readers for class tomorrow.

September was a hot month so all the windows were open. Sometimes a nice breeze would come in but most days were just hot. Mom made me a few sundresses and that helped she said when it got cool she would put the sleeves on them. I loved October all the leaves would start turning colors. On the week-end I would look for the ones that were pretty and put them in a book. Mom would ask how my leaf book was coming. One day Emma came over and I was gluing some in my book, she told me to bring the book to show and tell next week. After school I would go and see Honey, I would feed and water her and talk for a while. She was looking good. The vet was here today and said around the 20th we would have a colt. I would see her every day and she was moving kind of slow. On the 12th she was standing with her head down and breathing hard, didn't want her carrot or apple. I ran to the house for mom. Something is wrong with Honey she is sick. We went to the barn, mom said she would call the vet to stay with her. Keep talking to her she yelled for the boys. They seemed to know what to do and had her laying down by the time the vet got there. The vet called Mr. Anderson for help. Then doc told me to go into the house. No Honey was my pony and I will stay and talk to her. The colt's legs were under it so she was having a hard time. The vet had to reach in there and turn the colt, mom said sometimes it works, sometimes not. Stu was in the house with the boys so mom could stay with me. Mom said we may lose one or both of them. My heart was breaking, I went into the stall and sat by Honeys head and told her everything was going to be alright. I could see in her eyes she was scared. I just keep talking about how good she would feel when this was over. And she didn't have to do this again. Soon doc had the hind legs out but the front were still under it. Mr. Anderson held the back legs and when a sharp contraction started doc told him to pull slowly. You could see the butt coming the vet said stop. Let's see if she will push now. She was breathing hard and did push, doc helped her a little and soon we had a colt. But Honey just laid there she was so tired. So Mr. Anderson cleaned the colt and doc took care of Honey. I sat there talking to her telling her she had a good looking son and soon they would be up and eating. The colt made a sound and Honey rolled over some and looked at him. She started pushing on him to stand up doc said that was normal. Doc said let her rest and sleep some, the colt was eating and that was a good sign they were all leaving. The boys would be there and knew what to do, they talked to their dad and he told them to call if needed, doc would be back in the morning to see them. When I went to supper they were both sleeping the colt was up by Honey and her head was down by him, Stu said he was watching them. It was late and I had homework to do so I had to get it done. The boys said they would call me it things changed. So homework, bath and bed.

After I dressed I ran to the barn. They were both on their feet and Honey was eating. I called her and gave her two carrots. Told her what a good girl she was and I was proud of her. She had a nice son too. I went to eat and then the bus was coming. I ran to the mail box and he stopped for me. Told Emma about Honey and I still got my homework done. They will come over Saturday to see them. When I got home from school I asked mom if Emma would have to do that. She said yes but it isn't that bad for women. They can tell the doctor what is going on and do as he says. I was happy to know the doctor didn't have to pull the baby out. Everyday Honey was getting better so we put them out in the yard. The doc said to just let them be they were fine. I showed my leaf book at school and that gave the teachers an idea, that week-end all the kids were to find a few leaves and bring them to school Monday we would paste them on paper and hang them on the walls for our open house November 5th. Things were coming along fine. For the open house we had our moms make some cookies and punch. We showed our parents what we have been doing in school and our papers. I had B's and C's on my work that was good. While we were eating our cookies Mrs. Walker stood up and said she would like to introduce the teacher that was going to help while Mrs. Lawrence was on leave. Her name is Miss Carol Canning, she was young about twenty one and shy, she would be working with Emma till she went on leave. This way Miss Canning would get to know all of us. There were 3 kids in Kindergarten, 7 in first, 5 in second and 5 in third. She said there were too many kids to work with till she saw Mrs. Walker's group. She had 47 kids. On the way home Emma said she hopes Miss Canning would stay till she could return. Soon we would be off for five days the weather was getting cold that was when Emma started her leave. Miss Canning was a good teacher and will be okay when Emma is on leave. We all liked her and that helped. Thanksgiving was next week. The last day of school Emma wasn't doing well. Mr. Owens had to help her on and off the bus. On the way home Emma's back was hurting and she was not feeling well so I got off the bus with her. I wanted to be sure Frank was there to help her. Frank was there so I walked home.

Chapter 11

$\mathcal{S}$INCE MOM HAD THE BOYS she was happy. Larry still took her to the church dance and sometimes out to a movie and dinner. Lee and Stu were great sitters and we loved it when they went out. Thursday was Thanksgiving and we started to bake up a storm, Uncle Ray was bringing a ham and Uncle Roy the turkey with the stuffing and gravy. Frank called and said he was taking Emma to the doctor Saturday and would call when they got home. She would have the pies ready by Wednesday mom said that was fine. Peter was trying to help make cookies for the kids that was the first job I had at his age. Since he was now four he could help. We had a small party for him last Saturday for his birthday and he loved the things we gave him. Mom made him some new shirts and coveralls and I made a scarf and mittens for him. Lee and Stu made a train for him. He had a good time. Now he was baking, there was sugar and flour all over the kitchen. Mom didn't yell so I stayed quiet. We just helped him get done, had lunch, then off to bed for his nap. Frank called just after supper, Emma was in the hospital. They were the proud parents of a 7lb.4oz baby boy, his name was Ralph. Both mom and baby were doing fine Emma was worried she wouldn't be able to do the pies. Mom said we will get them done don't worry, just be here for Thanksgiving. Thanksgiving Day Larry was there early to help with the tables and benches. As soon as the Anderson boys were done with their chores they went home with their family. I checked on Honey and the colt. It was starting to get cold and I needed to be sure they were warm. Larry went with me, we started talking and he asked when I was going to name the colt. I said I'm not going to. If we sell him at market the new owner will want to do that. He asked if I was sure I wanted to sell the colt, yes I only need Honey. Well how about if I buy him for Peter, he is four and next year they will both be able to be trained to ride. Then he can name the pony. Will Mr. Brown let you have a pony, no but I can ask your mom if I can board him here. I told him I would think about it and let him know. People started arriving and we went into the house. As we were setting out food Frank and Emma came in with Ralph. Mom was the first to hold him then he was passed around. Larry brought in the cradle from the boys room and Ralph was laid down to sleep while we ate. All the food was good, after dishes were done the folks had their business meeting, it was a good year for all. Then they started planning for the spring planting. They set the date to buy the seed and hoped for an early planting season. After the meeting the men went out to look at the farm and the ladies started working on Christmas. Where and what each would make, Emma asked if we could all come to their home for Christmas that for the last two years they have been asked to join us and now it was their turn. That would be fine but we would do all the baking and cooking she would still need her rest. This would be the first time we would not be at a family's house. Uncle Ray said he would send the tree. That was set so now we had dessert. Then everyone started to leave, my uncles pulled mom aside and told her the boys were doing a great job, then they asked her a few questions and gave her a big hug. Soon all were gone but Frank and Emma. Frank and Larry went out to milk the cows and feed the animals. As they were feeding the animals the boys came back. Sorry they were late but at the last minute Lee told the family he was getting married in the spring to Sue May Peterson. They would talk to mom tomorrow. It was getting late and I was tired so I told mom I was going to bed. I must have gone right to sleep because I didn't hear anyone leave.

In the morning after Peter went to play I told mom what Larry said about the pony, yes he talked to her too. What was I thinking about doing? I could keep him if I wanted he was mine. I just said I wasn't sure yet I would let her know first. She told me that Uncle Ray knew a farmer that had a small pony he put out for breeding and if I wanted Honey to have another colt we would talk to him. I'm not sure Honey wants to do that again I would have to think about it. I had so much to think about. Saturday mom didn't have the boys so we went shopping for Christmas stuff. We needed a lot of yarn, thread and cloth for our gifts this year. I was making Larry and the boy's scarfs, hats and gloves my knitting was getting very good. I was making more ornaments for our tree too. I found a nice scarf and hankies for mom and I would cross stich them. I would say they were for my aunts. I would make a bigger blanket for Ralph too. We took all our stuff home and the boys left for town after supper. We had church tomorrow and mom asked about the pony, I'm selling him to Larry. We went into the sewing room and starting working, mom asked me if I liked Larry and the boys, yes why? Then I looked at her and you could see the smile and look in her eyes that I haven't seen in a long time. Would you mind if they all came to live with us. I asked mom what she meant. Larry asked me to marry him and I told him I had to talk to you first. I asked her if she loved him and she said yes she did. I wanted to know if I have to call him dad, no not if you don't want to. I said I would talk to him at church and then let her know. After that it was time for bed. We were early for church and met Larry and the boys when they got there. I told him we needed to talk now so mom took the boys into church and we sat in the car. I looked at him and asked if he loved mom. At first he just looked at me and then said yes and I love you too. Do you want to live with us? Yes, and marry mom? Yes, do I have to call you dad, only if you want to. Okay you can get married, but I can't sell you the pony, If Peter is going to be my brother I will give it to him. But don't tell him let me do it okay. Are you sure? Yes now let's go tell mom. We walked into church and mom was sitting with Frank and Emma, I walked over and said yes you can get married. I'm taking my brother Peter to Sunday school, I took Peter's hand and left.

After church Frank and Emma sat with us while mom and Larry went to talk to the pastor, we were going to their house for lunch and talk about Christmas. They came out of the office and said they would be getting married January 10th 1929 at 1:00 just family and a few friends. That was six and a half weeks away and Paul's birthday was a few days later. I was going to be a big sister. We had lunch and the ladies talked about the wedding. Then mom called my uncles and told them the date and time, they were happy for them. They would help with the food and the church. My aunts would be over to talk about how many people and what food mom wanted. When we got home I took Peter out to see Honey and the pony, we sat by the gate and watched them eat. I asked him if he knew what everyone was talking about. Yes sort of. My dad and your mom are getting married and we will live here with you. Now she will be our mom too. Yes that is right. So what would you call Honeys baby if you had to name him? Oh you mean Scout, Is that what you call him? Yes watch, he stood up and called here scout and the pony came right to him, just like Honey did to me. So I told him that Scout was now his pony for keeps and next summer he will be able to learn to ride him. He gave me a big hug then went running to the house yelling I have a pony. I went in to help mom start supper it was already 5:00. As I set the table I could hear Peter telling Larry that he was happy, he was going to have a real mom again and so was Paul. Even if Paul didn't know it yet. But his big sister gave him a pony all his for keeps. Mom just smiled at me and that made me feel good.

Chapter 12

NOVEMBER 30TH 1928 WE WERE back in school. Miss Canning was helping the third graders with their spelling and first and second were doing their readers. The Kindergarten were taking their nap. When they got up we would start working on our Christmas gifts for our families. It was some kind of craft Miss Canning had for us. First we made cards, we cut out snowmen and glued them to colored paper. Then the tree and the house. We could write what we wanted on the inside. Then we were given Popsicle sticks and yarn showed how to make snowflakes, then put a family name on them. Miss Walker came over to see our work and I ask if I could make one for Larry and the boys? Yes she went and got more sticks. After we made them we put glitter on them so they shined and the names were pasted on top. We hung them around the room on a string the teachers put up. We would take them home last day of school, Miss Canning had wrapping paper to wrap them in. Every day we made something. The last day of school it started to snow. Not bad only three to four inches. It looked so pretty outside. When we pulled up to the house a police car was there. I ran in looking for mom, are you and the boys okay. Yes just go take off your coat and boots. Everything was fine. Mom sat at the table and Lee and Stu came in, she told them the trial was over and Bill was gone for good.

Larry and Frank were working on the two small bed rooms for the boys. Peter would move up right after the wedding, for right now he would take his naps here. That was so he would get use to the room. Peter got to pick out which room he wanted and Paul would have my old room. Mom and I made curtains and blankets for them. Emma helped. Peter got a new bed and dresser so did Paul. Mom and Emma were on the sewing machine all the time. I had my Christmas presents done, and still working on mom's hankies. Two days of school left and seven days till Christmas. Everything was getting here fast, the wedding was in sixteen days. We had our party at church, I got a blue handmade scarf. It was so soft so nice I loved it. Peter got a car and Paul got blocks made of cloth. Uncle Roy brought our trees to church and Frank took ours home so he could cut and find the stand for it, the boys would bring it in tomorrow and then when Larry got there we would put the ornaments and lights on. It started to snow again and I was glad we were home. We were out of school till the 3rd of January 1929. Christmas was Wednesday so we took our gifts for the others over to Frank's house. The ones for our family we left under the tree. Mom made candied carrots and the ham, Plus the breads, rolls and cakes for the church boxes. So we were very busy all week. The way it was snowing I was worried about Larry and the boys making it out here. The roads were bad and if the farmers didn't clean the drives and our country road you wouldn't get down our way. You could hear Frank and the boys working on our end of the road. The milk man said that the egg man was a house or two behind him and most of the road was pretty good for now but we were getting more snow. Well if they made it so would Larry. About an hour later they were here. They got stuck twice but a few farmers helped pull them out. Glad they made it. We packed the car and off we went. My uncles made it and soon we had the food on the tables and were eating. We kids went to play or nap and the adults had their meeting. Then gift time. So many toys and clothes. I got two sweaters, a doll, three pairs of jeans and sox plus new boots. My uncles left early because of the roads. The snow was still falling and our road was bad, but as soon as they got to the highway they would be fine. When we got home the boys had the drive cleaned out. The snow was coming down fast and heavy, that's why the boys were back early. After soup and sandwiches we went in to the front room and Larry turned on the lights. They lit up the room and it was beautiful and nice and warm in here. Larry passed out the gifts and I gave them the ones from school. We opened them first, as we opened the snowflakes we hung them on the tree. The lights made them shine so bright and I was glad I got to make them each one. There were games and toys. I got a new coat with a hood, long pants and new shoes too. I was set for winter. I also got a pretty green dress for the wedding. It was like mom's that made me happy. Only sixteen days to go till the wedding then we would be a whole family.

It was snowing real hard so Larry and the boys stayed overnight. Larry took my room and I slept with mom. In the morning it was still snowing so Larry helped the boys in the barn. When he came in I asked about the ponies, Larry said he gave them an extra helping of oats for Christmas. I thanked him. They stayed over the week-end. Larry went home Sunday he had to work on Monday. He left the boys, and said if you need me call, he would try and make it out if he could. When he left it was the first time I saw them kiss and hug each other, then me and the boys. It snowed off and on all week, Larry made it out for dinner twice. Wednesday was New Years and he would be off for a few days and wanted to stay here so he could work on the rooms upstairs. We could all help and then take down the tree and put things away. Peter and I made pictures for his walls like mine. Mom and I made the curtains and mom his quilt, sheets were done and the room was ready. Monday Larry went back to work. Frank would go to Mr. Browns place and help Larry get rid of the things he didn't want or need any more. He gave a lot of stuff to the church for the needy then brought their stuff here. Monday Mrs. Anderson called to ask her to come and help her with some curtains for her front room she couldn't get them to fit right. Frank stayed with us and the boys took her over there. It was a surprise shower for her. Twelve ladies were there. She got a lot of nice things, most gave her baskets of canned goods now that she would have more mouths to feed. Wednesday we got a call the Lord's farm was on fire. The boys went to help like all the farmers did. When the boys came back they said all was lost. Thank God the kids were in school, Mr. and Mrs. Lords were fine. Didn't know how it started. First the house then the wind sent it to the barn. They got the animals out in time. We could see the smoke from school, then Mrs. Lord came for the kids and told the teachers they wouldn't be back, they were going to go to Illinois where her folks lived and stay with them. They had a big farm and needed the help. The ladies from church found clothes for them and helped with the trip. They stayed at the church till Friday and the farmers were buying their stock we got three cows, six ducks, and a horse. Also five sows but mom said no to the goats. By Friday everything was sold and they were on their way. It was a hard week and tomorrow was the wedding. The ladies went and cleaned the church and made it ready for us.

Larry stayed with Frank and Emma for the night. January 10th 1929 we were to be at the church at 12:00 and Frank and Larry were to be there at 12:30 but upstairs with the pastor. Mrs. Anderson was taking care of the boys, when it started Pastor, Larry and Frank came out the side door and went to the Cross. Then Peter and I walked up to the front and sat with the family. Next Emma came in she looked lovely in a green dress almost like mine. Then the music changed and the back doors opened everyone stood and looked to the back. Mom looked like an Angel they started down. Then something happened, I could see daddy and he was holding a little boy about three it was Sammy they were happy for her. As mom reached me she smiled and when I looked back they were gone. I watched as the Pastor said all the words, then we sang a song while they prayed to God. I was praying too. I did want them to be happy. So Pastor Louis turned to us and said I am pleased to present to you Lawrence and Mary Larson and family. I now had a new dad and two brothers, and the boys had a new mom. We went into the basement and for a luncheon put out by my uncles and ladies of the church. After we ate mom and Larry left, they were going to stay at a hotel in town they would be back Monday. They would call tonight before bed to say goodnight. Ann was going to stay with us. She was nineteen and getting married in June 2nd 1929. We had a good time with her and before you knew it they were home. Ann had dinner going before she left and things were back to normal. All of Larry's things were in mom's room so I guess that is where he will sleep. After supper they gave us some little things they picked up while they were gone. Then off to bed, mom came into my room and said my prayers with me. We talked she said she was happy, was I? I told her yes I was happy for her. Then I told her I saw daddy and Sammy at the church and they were happy too. She kissed me good-night and went to the door as she was closing it she looked at me and said I love you Sara and I said I love you to mom.

Chapter

13

JANUARY 17ᵀᴴ 1929. WE HAD Paul's first birthday party, mom made him a cake and he was having a ball with it, in his hair on the floor and anyone that got to close to him. Peter and I stayed away. The rest of the month snowed off and on. Our road was still bad so the farmers were going to the county meeting on February 3ʳᵈ to see what could be done. It started snowing the first of February and snowed till the 9ᵗʰ. We had no school the bus driver said he wouldn't try to drive down our road. Larry had a hard time getting back and forth to work he had to stay in town two times and wasn't happy. We didn't make it to church and I wanted to talk to dad. Snow or no snow the sheep and pig were going to start having their babies that would give us almost two months to fatten them up for market. Easter was the second week of April so that helped us. We were selling our milk to the dairy so mom didn't want to keep to many calves so far we only had ten but a few were still waiting. So far we had eighteen lambs, but more were coming around three or four every day. All lambs would go to market. The egg man came twice a week for the eggs he even had a sled with bells on it so if the snow was too heavy he would still make it here. His two golden brown horses were big. Frank and Larry went to the board meeting and Emma came over, Ralph was getting big. Paul liked to get on the floor and play with Ralph, I don't know what they said but they were laughing and playing like they knew what was said. I was helping Peter with learning to write his name and ABC's like Emma helped me. Mom and Emma were talking about the farms and how nice to have a man to help. Mom was going to have Larry go to the market and she was staying home with the boys. No market, I have been saving my money to go to the market. It's not fair. I told mom I was tired and went to bed. I was sleeping when she came in to say good-night. Larry told us in the morning that this year the county was going to pave the road and when it snowed the plows would take care of it.

Soon we were crating chickens and the rest of the animals. So far all we had was rain so the roads were fine. Friday night mom told me to take a bath and wash my hair, Emma was going to pick me up at 6:30 when she dropped off Ralph, and did I have my list ready yet? No but it won't take me long. After my bath while mom and Larry were talking mom brushed my hair. When she was done I went upstairs and made my list then went and showed it to her. She was pleased and asked if I had my money in my bag? Yes and I gave it to her, she counted all the change and added it up then she put two dollars in change back in it and the rest of the change in the cookie jar she took out some bills and put them in my bag. Make sure Emma or Larry are with you when you want something you know how the venders will cheat you. The men took the animals and Emma and I shopped. I got two soft toys for Paul and Ralph, a small train for Peter. Yarn, cloth, paints, paper and a straw hat for Larry. Then we found the vender with the patterns, I got thread and needles for mom plus cloth and a pattern to make Ann's wedding gift. I was making four place mats and four napkins. The pattern had apples and a tea set on it, I was sure she would love them. That was all I needed for the day and soon Emma was done too. We were tired so as soon as we packed the trunk we went looking for the men. Uncle's stock was sold so was mom's, Frank was at the end of his sale. Things went pretty good for all of them, Larry was learning that there is a lot to being a farmer. Even part time was hard. I gave him his hat, now he looked like the rest of the men. He picked me up and kissed my check and said thank you and a big hug. I sure will need this, he had a big smile on his face the rest of the day. Emma and I got home before the men so I showed mom what I bought. Told her who got what and showed her the pattern and cloth for Ann's stuff. She was proud of me. Just then the men got here and Larry came in and showed mom his hat and told mom I gave it to him now he is like the other farmers.

We had two weeks till Easter, the boys started shearing the sheep. I took Peter out to see what they were doing, they had two of their brothers over to help. Mom still had over sixty sheep and that was an all day job. As they sheared the sheep they had to bag it then weight it, then number the bags and add them in the book for mom. At supper Stu told mom she had more sheep then she thought there was still twenty-three more to do and they would have them done tomorrow morning with these she has eighty-four. How many did she want for the freezer? My uncles would come for the large animals and the boys would take care of the small ones. Uncle Ray would butcher them and bring them back. Mom said two cows, three hogs and eight sheep. The boys will do the ducks and chickens while I'm in school and the boys napped. This year mom had to make two hams, dinner rolls, three pies and jars of applesauce and pickles. Easter morning the hams were done, rolls and pies were packed and the jars were all in the car. Larry helped mom with the boys and mom did my hair. We did have a nice service and mingled outside for a few minutes I ran over to see dad and Sammy said Happy Easter and I bet God was having a big party and was glad to have his son back home. I told dad I really liked Larry and he was always very good to me. I wanted to know if he would be hurt or upset if I called Larry dad. I know you can't come here and tell me but if you would find a way to say yes or no. I will never forget you or Sammy, you know that too. I just don't want to hurt you so please help me. Thank you and have a nice dinner with Jesus. Everyone is at the car so I have to go I will see you next week. We set out for Uncle Ray's house and it was a nice warm day. Aunt Carol put out colored eggs and we had to find them, Joan helped Paul and we were told not to go by him. We had a good time, Mark and Peter each found seven eggs and I had four. We took them to Aunt Carol and she gave each of us a basket and it had a soft animal in it with candy. We played lots of games it was so nice outside. Then we ate. Soon it was time to go home, on the way home mom and Larry talked about the planting coming up. He told the families he would try and get some time off work but this was tax season and they were very busy. They told him to just do his job and help on the week-ends and this fall not to worry it would get done. When we got home it was early to bed, school tomorrow. Mom called Emma and Frank to say Happy Easter from all of us, she asked if John was here to stay now? No he was going to go back and pack up his things and sell the house. He may have someone that wants it, we will have to wait and see. When it sells he will be back for good. She was so happy. Even though he was sick he wanted time to do some farming so Emma started the family garden with things he wanted and they should have a good start by the time he comes back. He was so happy.

Chapter 14

*M*ONDAY THE BUS WAS ON time, Emma had two days left of leave. We still had nine weeks of school. By noon it started to rain so we had to eat lunch inside. It was a light rain so I knew the tractors would still be working our fields. Then it rained for a week, now they had to wait for the land to dry to go back to work. Saturday they were back at work, they worked all day and half the night. Only ladies and kids were in church, mom said God understood and they would all be back next week. I went to see dad and Sammy. The flowers Larry and I planted were starting to grow, I was happy to see that and told dad Larry helped me get them. Other people were putting flowers out too. It was starting to look nice in the yard. I will have to show Larry next week. We have to get going the girls have to get back to get the food on the tables for the farmers for lunch. We went and helped Aunt Carol, most of the food was taken over in the morning with the men, so all we had to do was help set it out and make coffee. The men washed up, fixed their plates and sat to eat. Larry told me that the hat really helped today. It was so hot and his face and neck didn't burn. The men said they would be done in an hour or two and would be home for supper, so when they returned to work we packed up our stuff and said good-by to Aunt Carol then left. I had school and Larry had work so he would be able to get some good sleep.

Mom made pork chops, potatoes, corn, and salad for dinner. As we were eating Lee told mom he would be leaving at the end April so he could work on his house before the wedding. We would be getting an invitation soon. Stu was staying and Hank would like to take Lee's place if mom said okay. What did their dad say about it? Fine with him if okay with her. He still had four boys at home, so mom said fine. Stu was dating Miss Canning so we will have to see were that goes. Ann was getting married and so was Lee, mom and I had to get busy on gifts. After homework we would set in the sewing room working on our gifts. Sometimes Emma came over to sit with us. Mom ironed my transfers and picked out the colors soon I was on my way. I would be done in no time. Still didn't know what to make for Lee's wedding, didn't know his girlfriend so don't know what she likes. Mom said we girls will go into town and see what we can find out and get something for them. She will call Mrs. Anderson and ask her too. We have six more weeks of school.

That Monday Emma brought Ralph over for mom to watch, this was her first day back to school. She would get on the bus with me and come home with me. When we got to school all the desks were moved. Miss Canning was staying and she would have grades k-2nd, Emma would have 3rd-5th and Mrs. Walker 6th-8th. I still had Miss Canning but since the classes were smaller she would have more time to work with each of us. One morning as Mrs. Walker called the room to order and each teacher called roll call she made her announcements this year the county was having a spelling bee the last week of school.

Each school was to send the top two spellers from each class to the county that week. So we will had spelling tests every Friday and the two with the lowest score was out. At the end the top two would go so we were to take our spellers home and study. I was doing well in spelling but my English was down, Larry was helping me and it was going up. Notes were sent home so the folks knew what was going on. Well my birthday was just around the corner and school went two more weeks into June because of snow days. We had a party for just family and friends. The Andersons were there and there was some talk that Lee was having problems with the house and his girlfriend, so please don't get anything till they say it is okay. It was hard to think I was seven years old. I opened my presents and I received many nice things, lots of yarn, cloth and a few new dresses. One was yellow and had daisies on it. It was for Ann's wedding I was the flower girl. Aunt Carol asked why daisies? Ann said it just jumped out at her. And she liked it. Two weeks before school was out and I lost the spelling bee. We had our two that would go to county next weekend. Suzie Parker and Rose Butler. I wished them both good luck. We would find out Monday who won, the teachers from each class had to go and when Emma came to pick up Ralph she didn't say a word. There were twenty nine schools in the county so there were fifty eight kids in each class so it took all day. Sunday I went to tell dad that I was doing well in school and to pull some weeds. I found a daisy and called Larry over, did he plant the daisy? No but a seed may have been mixed in with the pack. Maybe dad was saying he was proud of you Sara. We went home and had lunch then put on our work cloths and went to the garden to pull weeds I found two more daisies mom said she didn't put flowers in with the beans so Larry helped plant them in the front flower garden. There I found 6 more I told Larry I had a headache and was going to lay down for a bit. He said okay maybe too much sun. I washed and went to my room. Later mom called me for supper, I just listened to them talk and then helped mom with dishes. Are you feeling okay Sara? Yes I'm fine. After we were done I asked Larry if he would go with me to check on the ponies. We went and I asked if we could talk, I told him I didn't have a headache but needed time to think. I told him I asked dad for a sign if it was okay if I called him dad. I think my dad was telling me it was okay with him and Sammy if it was okay with Larry, so is it okay with you? How do you know Sara that it's okay? Well I told my dad how good you have been to me, and if he would tell me yes or no. Today he said yes, you see he knows I love Daisies and he put them were I would find them. You and I were the ones that put them all together so he said yes. When I looked at Larry he was crying he put his arms around me and said he would love for me to call him dad. He always wanted a little girl and now he had one, only one thing. You must never forget your dad or Sammy do you understand Sara. I had a real dad and he would keep telling me he loved me too. He held me for a while and it felt good. So we went to see the daisies and thank dad, as we got near we saw so many daisies, we both started crying and we thanked God and dad for this gift. Then we called mom she had just put the kids to bed so she came out. She looked at the garden and at us Larry said he would explain later. We had English to do before bed. School would be out in one week and his little girl was going to pass. Right Sara, right dad. As we went into the house mom stayed in the garden I could see she was crying. After English I had my bath and mom did my hair. We had one week left of school. Dad took me up to bed and said good night, he said he told mom what happened and she was happy for us. Then mom came up said my prayers and she went to leave. As she was closing the door she looked at me and said I love you so much Sara and I told her I love you to mom. Then she closed the door. I looked out the window and Thanked God and dad for their help. I told dad I would always see him on Sunday and I was still his little girl.

Monday we were told that no one from our school made first place but Rose came in second and Suzie came in fifth we were proud of both of them. Some of the kids in the other groups did well too. The last day of school, we had to clean out our desks. The teachers gave us brown bags with our names on them and so we got started, then we had our cook out. We had hot dogs and beans. Mr. Owens made them. We had potatoes salad, chips, ice cream and cake. Then the teachers called for each class to stand in their lines. We played games and ate more food. Soon it was time to go home. Mrs. Walker called all of us to stand in our classes with our brown bags. She told all of us that she was proud of us this year. Then she said when your name is called you will get your report card and go to your bus. Mr. Owens was there waiting for us. Kindergarten went first then each grade at a time. It was hard to say good-by to some of your friends not sure who would move or who would be back next year. When my name was called I got my report card and got on the bus. I couldn't wait to get home. As soon as I got off the bus I ran all the way to the house for mom. She met me at the door. I gave her my card and then she smiled and said "Sara Cross passed to the second grade." I was so happy I asked if I could be the one to tell dad, yes when he comes home. When I heard his car I ran out yelling I passed to second grade. He picked me up and gave me a big hug. He said he was proud of me. We went inside so he could read my card. I had a B plus in English and all A's in the rest of my grades. I was happy. At dinner I told Stu and Hank they said it was great. Then they said that Lee wasn't getting married. Sue May's family didn't like the house. Mr. Peterson said he was sending a crew out to take it down and build a larger and nicer house for his little girl or Lee could come to work for him and he would get them a house in town. Lee said she knew what he was doing and didn't say anything when she would come and look at it. Then he told Mr. Peterson that he would have to talk it over with Sue May and let him know tonight when he brought her home. He told her he was a farmer he had over 100 acres and his family was helping him stock it. He would not work for her dad, she said she wanted nice things not homemade stuff. That he didn't really love her if he wouldn't take a job with her dad and move to a new house in the city. He said he was staying here so did she want this life or not it was up to her. No new house, things would stay the way they were if she wasn't happy then the wedding was off. Stu said she gave him his ring and asked Hank to take her home. Lee was still going to work on his farm and get on with his life.

What a year 1929 was, mom got married and I had two brothers a new dad and I was seven and in second grade. Ann's wedding was this Saturday and I was the flower girl. I still had three days to finish her gift. Summer was now here. The day of the wedding mom helped me wrap the gift. I was so proud of it. I had to be at the church at 1:00 to get my hair done and dressed, so dad took me over. The rest of the family would come at 2:00. Ann had a basket of rose petals and Daisies in it and a necklace with a heart on it. They put half of my hair in a ponytail and then made curls around it, the rest had curls hanging down. When that was done I put my dress on and someone was taking pictures of me. Ann put a crown of Daisies around the curls. I looked like a princess, I wanted to cry. Ann told me again what to do, I was to walk with Willis he was the ring bearer down then we were to stop and have a picture taken, then were to drop the flowers petals. I would then go to the spot where I was to stand. When we walked back I was to put my hand on his arm and stop for pictures then too. I think I got it. At 1:45 everyone but the bridal party went upstairs. Then the pastor came down to pray with us and said it was time to go up. He would see us upstairs. We got in line and started up, we met Uncle Roy at the top. He gave Ann a real big smile and hug. The music started and Ann gave me a nod to go. I did as I was told and stopped at my spot. Mom and dad sat there smiling at me. Then the rest of the girls came down. The music changed and everyone stood up and looked to the back. The doors opened and Uncle Roy and Ann started down, I looked at James and he was all smiles. Then I could see Uncle Roy and Ann. As they got to the front Uncle Roy gave her a kiss and put her hand in James hand, then turned to sit with Aunt Carol she gave him a hug as he sat down. He had a tear rolling down his cheek. Pastor did the service and Willis gave them the rings as they were asked for. At the end Pastor Louis turned them to the people and said "On June 2nd 1929 I'm proud to present Mr. and Mrs.

James Parker." Everyone clapped then Ann nodded to Willis and me and we went to stand in front. I took his arm and we started to the back, we stopped for the pictures and then we stood where we were told. James and Ann came next then the rest of the party. The people were next to come out of the church. Lots of hugs and kisses, we were told to smile and say thank you to everyone. As the people were done they went to the basement and we went back into church for more pictures. I was glad it was over. Ann said after we eat I can go tell dad how I did and show him my dress and hair. She said the basket and necklace were mine to keep as a gift. I thanked her and gave her a hug and kiss. Pastor Louis said grace and we ate, soon people were dancing and the music was playing they were having a good time. I went to see dad and Sammy. I told them I had a good time and showed them how I looked said I had to get back because I was to help with the gifts. I would see them tomorrow. Willis and I had to have a picture taken to look like we were dancing. We did some funny things and then a nice picture. We had lots of fun. Then they started opening their gifts, there were a lot of store bought things that is the changing of the times. Mom even gave her an Iron pot. Then she opened mine, she held them up for everyone to see and said Sara Crow made these for us and I love them thank you Sara, she was also my flower girl. I knew my face turned red. Some were starting to leave so mom said we had to go, we had a wonderful day but Pam was there watching the boys and we needed to get back. We said our good byes and left. I was tired and glad to rest. Mom said that as soon as Aunt Carol gets the pictures back she will bring them over and we can pick out the ones we wanted. She would order them for us and it might take up to four or five weeks to get here.

Chapter

15

*W*ELL SUMMER WAS HERE PETER was four years old but big for his age, so he was learning to ride. We went riding with the boys or dad I told mom next spring we could breed the ponies. She said she would let my uncles know. It was very hot, we worked in the garden and set out the wash. It didn't take long for it to dry. Mr. John sold his home and moved in with Emma and Frank. He had his garden and was so happy. It gave him something to do. One morning mom gave us new shorts and tee shirts to wear. Dad got them at the store and they were so cool. It was too hot for dresses. It was also too hot for me to go to market this time, but this was fine I had so much from my birthday that I gave a small list to Emma and she would pick it up for me. It was August and mom and I went to town, dad was with the boys. We did some shopping and then went to lunch at a soda shop. This was something new for me. As we were eating mom asked if I would like to have a new sister or brother. Why I asked, she looked at me and said she was going to have a baby and do I want a sister or brother. As long as you and the baby are okay I don't care. I remember last time and I would worry. There were a lot of things that happened, we lost dad and I fell down the stairs that was why your Aunt was there. This time I have all of you and I will be fine. I asked when the baby would be here, In February around the 12th. Good that will give me time to help with the baby clothes. We had to get home to make dinner and we were still working on my dresses for school Labor Day was two weeks away. We had seven dresses done. I like homemade dresses better than the store ones. You could bet no one had one like yours. Mom's dresses were always prettier I will be able to wear jeans and shirts to school this winter. Next market is in October and I need to go. I will need things for Christmas and for the baby.

Summer had gone fast the tractors were starting the harvest and I will start school next week. I was ready for second grade. The bus was on time and we picked up Emma, Frank was going to take Ralph to the doctor for his shots, then bring him to mom. As we started to go into the school so much had changed. The school board made a lot of changes over the summer. Two half walls were put in it looked like a pie cut in quarters, strange. The right corner was K-2 grade, the middle corner was 3-5th the left corner was 6th – 8th. All the classes faced the last corner where Mrs. Walker could watch all of us. We all had new books. Readers, spellers, arithmetic, English and history. Plus we all had new desks and each one had our names on them. This way we knew were to sit. Mrs. Lawrence told us to find our seats. Teacher told us on the inside of the book covers were ten lines. We are to write our names on the first line, the date and year. The condensing of the book is new. When school is out the board will look at the books. If you do not take good care of it the board will send your family a bill for a new one to replace the one you had. So if I were you I would take good care of my books. I took my books home so mom could help me put covers on them. Peter was in kindergarten and his books had to stay in school. September went fast we had a lot to learn. I really liked school. October was here and we will go to market. Mom stayed home and Stu and Hank would keep an eye on her. I went with Emma and we were coming back as soon as our shopping was done. We had mom's list and would get it first. Then we did ours. I needed cloth, there were some with colors so I got some yellow, green pink and blue. I could make a quilt for the baby and hit either sex. I found the yarn and patterns I wanted and things to make for Christmas. As soon as Emma was ready we said goodbye to the guys and left. We were home by noon. I helped mom with lunch and the boys said they took turns coming in and seeing what she was doing. Mom looked at me and laughed I was just glad she was okay. October started to get cold that meant a long cold winter with lots of snow and since the roads have been paved we should be able to get to town and school okay. Halloween we had a party at school. The parents made the treats we dressed up and played games and we had a good time. Emma was at the house when we got home so she could see us dressed up. Emma told mom she was going to have a twins in May or June. We were all so happy for them. More baby clothes.

November was here and mom started to look as big as the turkey and she still had three months to go. She was going to see the doctor tomorrow, dad took off work to go with her I wanted to go to but we had school. I would find out when I got home. It was a long day, on the bus Emma had to tell me to sit down twice. As we got to my stop I jumped off and started to run to the house. I stopped no car was in the drive. I turned to Emma, she took mine and Peter's hands and we walked to the house. I started to cry. Sara there is no reason to cry we don't know what is going on. When we walked into the kitchen mom was at the sink. I let out a yell and ran to her crying. Sara what is wrong, Emma told her and she sat down and hugged me, honey dad was called into work. So when we got home he left. Sara the doctor said I'm fine, but I'm going to have twins. That is why I'm getting so big. The babies will be here any time from January 20th to February 10th. All of us are fine so don't worry. When I go into the hospital you will be there, I promise. That made me feel better. One of the boys will come and get you, now Emma knows so they will let you out of school. I couldn't wait for Thanksgiving we will have five days off. The week of Thanksgiving we did a play just for the school, telling the story about the first Thanksgiving. It was a lot of fun and so funny. Tuesday the teachers said to have a nice time and not to eat too much turkey. We were staying home and the families were coming here Plus Emma and Frank. Mom was to stay off her feet so Emma and I made to rolls and pies. Larry and Frank did the turkeys and put up the tables. We were ready as soon as everyone arrived. Everyone was surprised at how well we did. We set out the food and we all ate. Our families seem to be growing and soon no one will have room for all of us. The adults said that Christmas was to be the last time we would all go to one house. Starting next year we would all stay home. If we had married kids they would go to the parents' home. For Christmas we will start giving gifts to only the kids under fifteen and we will be sure to take them over to their home before Christmas. This year will stay the same since most things are made or bought by now. A vote was taken and all agreed, mom said for last family get together it would be nice if it was in the old family home. Everyone agreed with her but she was to do nothing. That was fine. The rest of the month was fine I was waiting for snow but none was in the air. We were back in school Monday. Soon we will start on our Christmas gifts for home. We also had the party at church. The church board said this was the last year for presents. It was getting to costly but the food boxes would still go out. Dad took moms stuff over last week and he will for Christmas, what we didn't have he would get in town.

December seemed to warm up, it was still cold but nice. We still had tests because report cards came out in two weeks just before Christmas. We did a lot of studying and were sure we passed the tests. Only time will tell. Ten days before Christmas we took them home, they were to be signed and back in school Monday. I took it to mom the first thing when I got home. I was doing well, I had B's and C's. She said dad will have to start working with you again but this was very good. Emma got Ralph ready for home and asked how she was, tired but fine. Well Frank had talked to Mrs. Anderson and after the first of the year she will start watching all the boys. Ours and Ralph. Ann was going to come and stay all day with mom, and Frank will pick up the boys in the morning. This will be the time for her to rest and Ann will do the meals and keep house for her. Once the babies are here we will see what has to be done. Mom signed our cards and set it on the table for dad to see. Emma went home and I helped with dinner. We had lamb stew and rolls. Stu and Hank said they would be around close for the rest of her time. Everyone was taking care of her. At school we were working on a new ornament for our Christmas tree, we could make as many as we wanted but we had to do them right and show the teacher before we did a new one. We had fun and didn't do much school work. Some reading in the morning and spelling after lunch. But we worked hard on our gifts. We had round balls and could glue or paste anything we wanted on them, the teacher would put the name you wanted on it for you with a marker. I made stripes on some and stars or snowflakes. I had all the names of my family put on them. Next year I will have two more names. I was hopping one would be a girl dad had his boys so I needed a girl. Mom didn't go to the church party so I stayed home with her. We worked on our Christmas presents. She said dad was going to have to pick up things at the store for some of the family, she didn't have time to make all of the things needed. She made a list and gave it to dad before he left for work Monday. I would be out of school for the next two days. I helped mom with the meals and worked on the baby things. Now I had to make two of everything. I had the quilts done, and eight sleepers. I was working on buntings and only had six done. Mom had a lot of dippers so I didn't make them. She made small blankets and sheets for the cradles.

Dad took the food to the church and then we started on the things for our Christmas dinner. We were making two hams so that was easy to do. As before Emma and Frank were here early and we were ready. Dad lit the tree lights and we set the presents under the tree. As the families arrived they did the same thing. We set the tables and as we sat down Uncle Ray said he would like to take this time to read something he wrote for this last get together. He thanked the Lord for such a wonderful large family. We have all had good times and bad, but it is good to know that we will always have family to help us. Thank you Lord for keeping us all healthy and able to take care of others. Most of all thank you for this home where it all started and for this day, now grace, Lord Bless this food Amen. Everyone was quiet so he said let's eat. We had hams, beef roasts, turkeys and so much food I didn't think we would eat half of it. After all was cleaned up dad helped mom to the front room. We opened our gifts and everyone was pleased. There were a lot of store things and that was nice, but I like the home made things best. The women went to the kitchen and made mom stay where she was. I went in and they were wrapping food and putting it in our freezer, when mom has the babies she will need this for meals. She will need help for a few weeks and we will all take turns helping. I told them thank you and gave them a hug. They all started to leave soon after so mom could rest. The men had taken down the tables and put the chairs in the barn, the boys will put them up later. Mom went and laid down.

Chapter

16

NEW YEAR'S EVE WE WATCHED 1929 go out with a bang. 1930 was here we made popcorn and root beer and watched the fireworks from town out the window. Then off to bed. We still had four days off so we had time to work on baby things. I worked as hard and as fast as I could. Mom told me Sara, we have all the things we need, so slow down. I know you can't wait but they will be here soon. Why don't you start working on some wedding gifts, you know someone will be getting married this summer. Also a few things for Emma's twins. So that is what I did. The fifth of January we were back in school. Everyone had something new on it was nice. We all had sweaters, jeans, new hats and gloves. It looked like it may snow soon then we would go out and play in it at lunch time. By the 10th it did start and it was a heavy one we had 10 inches before school was out. Mrs. Walker said there would be no school tomorrow, she gave us notes for our parents. It snowed Saturday and Sunday. Thank God for the snow plows. Dad was able to get to church and home. On the 14th dad woke me up and said get dressed fast we are taking mom to the hospital. I put on my jeans, two shirts and my heavy pants plus wool sox. When I got down stairs Emma was there with Frank and Ralph. Dad was warming up the car then we would leave. Mom asked if I did as she said and I showed her all I had on. Good now put on your boots. Frank helped me with them as dad came in. I told you we would take you with us are you ready, Mom said yes. We got in the car and promised to call as soon as we could. We were off to the hospital. As soon as we got there they took mom away, I was scared till dad said they had to get her ready, then we will be able to see her. Open your coat and take off your hat. Give your hat and gloves to me and I will put them in my pockets. If you start to get warm take off your coat. Just then mom's doctor came into the hospital. Looks like we will have a few more babies soon as she is ready to go. Will we get to see her I asked, the doctor looked at me and said come with me. Dad and I followed him, as we got to a door he stopped and said when I say leave you go at once do you hear me? I said yes.

So tell her you love her and you will see her soon. Kiss her and leave okay and I did. It was hard but we went and sat in the waiting room. It seem like hours till someone came out for us. Dad was walking the floor and I was sitting on the bench when a nurse called dad's name. I jumped and we went to see mom. She was holding two pink blankets, two girls she said to dad do you mind. No as long as all of you are fine. Yes they are said the doctor as he came in the room. He looked at me and said I hear you were worried. I said yes but thank you for doing a good job. I walked over and dad picked me up so I could see them. They were all pink and pretty, but so small. I looked at the doctor and he said that when you have twins they are small but they were both 4lbs. 5 oz. You watch out they will grow like weeds. Mom asked us what we should call them so the birth certificates can be filled out. I looked at dad what do you want? You tell us what you want Sara. I looked at them and said this one looks like a June bug so let's call her June. This one looks like a pink rose so let's call her Rose. You two pick a middle name this was hard enough so their names are June Marie and Rose Marie. Dad said I could call home and tell them we have two girls and their names. I went to the phone and called. Frank answered and I told him everything. Most of the families were there because there was a lot of noise. I told them we would be home soon because mom and the babies need to rest.

Four days later dad, mom and Aunt Kate came home with my two sisters. Everyone was there to see them. I helped mom to bed. Aunt Kate was going to sleep in my bed and I would sleep on the couch. This would only be for a few days, till mom was feeling better. Then Aunt Kate stayed home, so Ann came to stay a few days. By the end of January mom was up and around, she had to go see the doctor so dad took her and Aunt Kate someone had to hold one of the babies and I wasn't that big yet. Doctor said all was well and mom can start slowly doing things. So Ann stayed home and started getting ready for her baby. It will be here in May. I told mom I made a quilt, three buntings and a blanket for Ann. I did them while working on June and Rose's things. We can send them to her later. Mom said she had a few things to finish for her too. The doctor was right and soon the girls were getting big. I learned to help change them and rock them to sleep. Mom and dad did most of the things but I was learning and did my best. Emma had her babies on April 6th 1930 and it was two boys, Michael and Robert. Miss. Patterson was taking her place because she was going to stay home with the kids. The girls were getting big. Before you knew it they were crawling, so the gate was put back up. Paul loved to play with them, he had a ball on the floor crawling around with them. I loved to hear them laugh. Peter liked them but they were girls and he wanted boys. I told him you have a brother now I have sisters. But Peter kept at it soon dad took Peter out for a talk. Things got better.

Chapter
17

WELL TWO YEARS HAVE GONE by it was 1932 Peter is seven and is going to the market with dad. Paul is four, the girls are two and I'm ten. The weather was changing and soon it was market and planting season. Our house was always noisy the girls were crying or the boys were fighting and mom had to take care of everything. One day I asked her if it was worth it, we used to have peace and quiet here now this, Sara, yes I love all of this, I have five wonderful children and a great husband. What more could I want. Yes, I see and I have two brothers and two sisters. I wouldn't give it up for the world. Stu asked Miss Canning to marry him. He had a home for her and everything was ready so she said yes. They were married on August 19, 1932. They had a small church wedding. Mr. and Mrs. Anderson had a party at their home after the service. I made them napkins and two table runners. We had to start looking for help. Hank has been working on his home and was seeing a girl, but he was not sure this is the one.

One morning Hank told mom he had a friend that was coming from Ohio. His name was Steve and he used to work on a farm, would mom talk to him and see if he could work here? She told Hank to have him come to dinner when he gets here and they would talk. Steve came to dinner on Sunday, mom, dad, Hank and Steve all went to the barn. They showed him around and where he would sleep. Hank and dad told him what he would be doing and how they wanted it done. If he wanted the job it was his, when could he start? Hank was staying at his house so he could keep working on it so Steve would stay in the shed. After chores they would go over to Hank's and help him. Things were going along fine and before you knew it 1934 was here. Time was passing and both boys were in school so mom only had the girls at home. That gave her time to do her garden and the canning when the time came. She would go to Emma's and Emma would come and help her. I would do what I could when I got home. Dad would help all of us with homework after dinner. Then chores. Peter and I had to help with the sheep and our ponies, Honey was in heat so I told mom we could breed her, she would call my uncles and find a breeder. Mr. Cane came to see the ponies. He had a black pony for honey and a black for scout to breed with so we said yes. The next day he brought them over. Honey was at one end of the barn and Scout the other end. The mare was put in with Scout and they were okay together. The black was put in with Honey and she didn't like it. Mr. Cane said he would be back in a few days and gave mom his card. For three days Scout was having a ball. Honey wasn't. Mom told the boys to cage her the next day after we went to town if they mated a time or two to let her go and take the male out. We went to town for the day and did a lot of shopping. Mom now used the grocery store for her flour and cornbread. She sometimes got Kool Aid and Kool pops. Sugar was on her list too. From there we went to the Hot Dog Stand and had lunch. With five kids that took time. Now the fabric store, this was the last year mom was going to make my dresses for school. She found all the new patterns and we picked the fabric for each of them. I would have six dresses, four skirts, six blouses and four neck scarfs. I was going to make the skirts and scarfs I was pretty good at sewing and loved it. When we got home Honey was in her pasture all alone. Mr. Cane came the next day to pick up the ponies. Good, I didn't like his ponies. He said he would call mom in two months to see how things were going and let her know how his mare was. This was July of 1934, it takes eleven months for a horse to have a colt so if Honey was having one, it would be here June of next year. That is a long time.

We started school right after Labor Day I was in 8th grade, Mrs. Walker was still our teacher. She did have two children but had them in the summer when school was out. So she never missed school. They went to school in the next town over where they lived. So we didn't know them. I loved all my new clothes, everyone had new clothes. 8th grade was hard, we had to get ready for high school and that was in town. It was a little scary. Dad helped me but I had to learn a lot myself. When dad was late or stuck going out of town for a few days. I would help mom with the boys. In October we heard from Mr. Cane, Molly would have her colt in June how was Honey? Not sure the vet will be here next week, we will let him know. Well the vet said yes she would have a colt in June, he would like to see her every two months. This was September so he would be back in November. School was going along fine, before you knew it Halloween was here, we were have a party on the 30th because it was a Friday. I helped mom with making the candy and treats for the kids. 8th grade helped with the party. We were getting ready to move up in the world, just like the last few 8th grade kids did. We still had plenty of treats.

Chapter 18

*N*OVEMBER WAS A COLD MONTH, I was glad we stayed home for Thanksgiving. Mom still sent things to my uncles every Holiday. There was a five day Holiday for Thanksgiving. The vet came to look at Honey. She was doing well and he was on his way to see Molly next. June was going to be a busy month, we will have to see which one would be first to have their colt. I didn't care who was first as long as Honey and baby were fine. It started to snow and went on for five days. The boys loved it and played outside after school as much as they could. I always did my homework first it was not easy. Our report cards came out the 14th of December and I wanted good grades. So far even with all the snow we had we didn't miss any days of school. The 14th we took our cards home and mom had to read the boys first because they were yelling me first, me first. So first was Paul's my how fast he had grown, he had B's and C's in all his grades. Very good Paul, Peter had A's and B's that was a surprise the way he acted in school. As soon as they heard their grades they went to play. So just mom and I were at the table. She opened mine and said well Sara you have two A's two B's and a C. The C is in History they are all good grades and with them you will pass into high school. Let's try and pick up that C before the next grading, dad will help all he can but with the boys needing help he has a lot going on. I know you will do it. At supper that night dad looked at the cards. He said we all had very good grades and on payday we would get our money. Sara I don't know much about history I wish I could help you more I'm sorry. That is okay dad I will see what I can do. Willis had started working for us, Hank had a lot to do with his farm going so well. Willis said he loved history and would be glad to help me if the parents were okay with it. Yes that would be fine. So after supper we sat at the table and he helped me by Christmas I felt better about school. The last week before Christmas we worked on the ornaments for home. 7th and 8th grades could make what they wanted. I made a wreath for the door and one family ornament for the family and one for me. After Christmas mine would go in my box in my room for my tree when I got married. That week mom and I did a lot of baking for the church and home. We packed up the things for church, Pastor Louis asked those that could please add something extra. There were a lot of families that needed help. So dad went to the store and got a case of corn, beans and peas. With his job and the farm we were doing okay so we helped. Mom and I still made homemade gifts for our family. Dad and mom still went to the store for things too. I love the ornaments we made every year. I had some from the store but most were homemade this year I will need a bigger box. Our tree was up and the little ones were waiting for the party at church. Pastor gave a nice service and then we went downstairs. We had lots of treats and games for them. Soon it was home to bed. Tomorrow was Christmas and mom and I still had things to wrap. At midnight mom said Merry Christmas Sara we have come a long way you and I. Yes we have mom, next year I will be in high school and before you know it I'll be in 12th grade then out. Where has the time gone? We went and sat at the table with our hot chocolate and talked for a while. From the time I was three till now we have gone from the two of us to seven in the family. We were all happy and healthy things were going good with the farm, dad loved to work on the farm, mom had her large family and I had a family. We went to bed after a hug and kiss, we said my prayers and I thanked God for all the things I had.

I woke to yelling so I knew the kids were up. I dressed and went downstairs. I told mom I didn't hear the girls get up so I'm sorry I wasn't down to help right away. Hank, Steve and Willis came in for breakfast said most chores were done. As soon as they could they would head for home but would be back for evening chores. We told them to come into the house after evening chores for pie and cake. Okay will do. Soon as we ate we went into the front room. Dad gave out the gifts and the kids went wild. Paper was everywhere. Mom and dad gave me a necklace with a heart with my name. It was so pretty, I had clothes and a new jacket, with gloves to match. Mom made them. The kids got toys and clothes and more toys.

It was a nice Christmas. After all was cleaned up mom and I started the ham for supper. We would had soup and sandwiches for lunch. I went to see Honey. We gave them all extra oats for Christmas, then we checked the sheep. We did our chores cleaned out the stalls and put down clean hay. Since it was cold we put more hay in the ponies stall. Honey was starting to gain weight. The vet would be back in January to see her. So far she was fine. We had supper and when the boys came in we gave them their gifts. They made toys for the kids, and gave me a necklace with a pony head on it. Hank told mom it was time he got married, his house was done long ago and Hope wanted to get married now. So he was getting married January 15th but Matt was taking his place here.

The first of the year was his last day. It was going to be a small wedding but we were invited. Please don't go to any trouble for us. After they left mom said aren't you glad you've been working on things for weddings now you just have to think what you want to give them. I had a lot of things so I asked mom if she would help me look and ask Mrs. Anderson what they would want or need. The next day mom called, they had a double bed, and not much for it. Good mom and I looked at the sheets and pillowcases I made, mom said they would be great, also a few dresser scarfs. Mom had a quilt she made and a blanket. We were set. It was hard to see that a new year was here in two days. New Year's Eve we made popcorn and had soda, cookies and milk and waited to see the fireworks at midnight. Before you knew it 1934 was gone and 1935 was here. We drank a toast to the New Year and put the little ones to bed. Then I went to help clean up from the party. Dad had most of it done so I helped mom. Soon I was in bed, the girls were sound to sleep. I was looking out the window when mom came in we talked for a few minutes then said prayers. She kissed me good night and left.

We went to Hank's wedding and party at Mr. Anderson's home. He cleaned out the barn and there must have been seventy people there. It was a lot of fun. They opened their gifts and were happy with the things we gave them. Hank gave mom a hug and kiss saying they sure will use the quilt and hugged me saying the sheets will sure help too, Thank you very much. Hope thanked us and said she would put out the dresser scarfs when they got back next week. Mrs. Anderson gave mom a box with food for supper in it, there was so much left over and the boys would be back for supper. We headed home at 4:00 the boys left for chores and we made supper. There was a lot of food, we will have sandwiches for lunch all week. Matt, Steve and Willis did a good job, and helped dad with taking stock to market. Peter and Paul would go with them. Sometimes I would go if mom and I needed something from there, sometimes the whole family went. Emma, Michael and Robert would go with us. Ralph was with Frank. The men folk, and the women folk were on their own. We had fun. In June Honey had a black colt he was a charm. I told Honey this was her last and she did a good job, Mr. Cane came to see the colt. Molly had a black and white colt and it was a girl. He asked mom if we would think of selling the colt to him he was a beauty. Mom called me over and told me what he said, no he's not for sale. He was already someone's pony not mine any more. So I'm sorry. He left not a happy man. Mom asked me who the pony went to. Why Paul of course. I can't give one to Peter and not Paul. So we called the boys over and I told Paul the pony is yours so you find a good name for him. Peter said he would help, I told him he had to wait a year for the guys to train him for riding but he could learn on Honey when the guys and dad had time. The boys would do our harvest and my uncles helped each other with their boys. Before too long cousins were get married and having babies. Steve left to go back home, his dad was not well and mom needed him. Our families were growing. The next thing you knew it was 1937.

Chapter 19

*H*ERE I WAS GOING ON fifteen and in high school. I had three years to go and dad and I had a talk, was I planning to go to college? I think so, I know it takes money and I have been saving. He said he would put me in for a grant from his company to help with the school, but I had to have good grades. So far I've had A's and B's, so I will apply for the grant. I told him I was hoping to be an accountant like him. I was doing great in math and loved numbers. Well we would have till next year to see what they say. I started going to football games. Went to the homecoming dance with a boy named Scott, but I was home most of the time. I used that time to study, I was the oldest and had to show the kids the right way. I wanted mom and dad to be proud of me. On Sundays I would go and talk to dad and Sammy, I would tell them about the friends I went to the games with, be most of all wanting to go to college. I wanted to go to Georgia State. It was 362 miles away and I would have to stay there. First I had to pass then pray for the grant.

One Sunday as I was going to see them something was wrong, their crosses were on the ground. I looked then called dad someone broke them off, you could see a lot were broken. Dad called the Pastor over and the police were called, I tried to put them back up but that didn't work, dad said Sara, Saturday you and I will take care of this. Dad called my uncles and told them what happened and that grandpa and grandmas were down too. Saturday we met them at the store, there were sixteen crosses broken and the sheriff was looking into it. A lot of families were here looking for new markers. Dad and I looked around we looked at crosses and angels, then just headstones. There were some that had names on them I asked dad if we could have a headstone with their names on it, just find the one you want. I saw one that I liked it had crosses and hearts with an angel in the middle. I asked dad how much it would cost. He went to ask, my uncles came over and said they found a nice one for the grandparents too. Dad came back and said the price would be $125.00 plus we had to pay for the words. I told dad I had $100.00 if he would help me I would pay him back. He said let's tell him what you want it to say, okay. So we talked to the man, I told him on the first heart I wanted it to say Samuel T Crow loving husband of Mary Crow Beloved Father of Sara and Sammy Crow, died April 19th 1925 the second heart was to say Sammy Crow Beloved son of Sam and Mary Crow Beloved brother of Sara Crow. Born May 17th died May 17th 1925. Dad paid him and said he would call us when it was ready to be set. As soon as we got home I gave him my money, let me know how much I still owe you. I gave him a hug and went to bed, I thanked God for sending Dad and the boys to us. We make a great family.

The man called and said the stone was ready and they would be at the cemetery Wednesday at 10:00 they had a lot to set so come when you can. Mom called my uncles, they were going at 10:00 we would meet them there. Mom and I were there early, we pulled weeds and planted flowers. As the men started to place the stone I told Mr. Miller it was the wrong one this one was bigger than the one I saw. He said the ones in the store were models this was the right size, it was beautiful so they set the stone, Mom started to cry, Sara you did a wonderful job it is great. She started crying more so I left her alone and went to watch them put the grandparent's stone up. When they were done we pulled weeds and planted flowers for them too. Then we all went home. Dad said he stopped after work and was pleased with the job, how did we like it? I loved it and so did mom they did a nice job. We had fried chicken and fried potatoes for dinner Matt and Willis sure loved to eat and so did Peter and Paul. I think we all loved chicken.

After mom and I cleaned up we went to the sewing room, we were teaching June and Rose to cross stich, Rose took to it right away but June liked to play so mom took her over by her and started her on making a quilt for a doll. Mom said it would be for her doll so she had to do a good job, which worked. Soon we were all working at something. Mom said I should start working on my hope chest, I told her that I have and would she like to take a look, we would Saturday after chores. That would be fun. So Saturday after lunch we went up to my room and looked at what I had, first my Christmas ornaments I keep them in my hutch Frank made for me, and then we opened my hope chest he made me, it was big. We took out two quilts and five dollies. Then napkins, table runners, two blankets, four sheets and pillow cases to match, six Towels and potholders and three rag rugs. So far that is all I have done. I still need sheets and pillow cases, I would like to have home made things for my house as much as I can. Mom was pleased your chest is almost half full. Where are the things you made for weddings? I keep them in a box on top of my hutch, so I showed them to her. It was full of a lot of things I said now a days girls want things from stores, and so I may keep them for me. Mom said yes you don't see handmade things too much anymore.

The summer of 1937 was hot we had the crops in and needed rain bad, our animals were breeding and we would have stock to sell but rain was needed to help feed them this winter, and grass to feed them now. I did a lot of praying Pastor said it would come with praying to God, it was in his time. No rain in June the kids had to stay in the house or barn. It was too hot for them in the sun. We did our chores then sat in the shade, some days there was a breeze and that was nice, July started the same way. Then one morning it was gray out mom told the kids to stay in the house, it didn't look good, the boys made sure the animals were safe. Mom told everyone that if she yelled we were all to head for the cellar there were two doors to the cellar one down the kitchen stairs and one on top outside, both were heavy doors and locked. We called Emma and she heard that a town was hit 60 miles south of us and the tornado was heading east south east, not our way but there could be more out there to listen to the radio so mom turned it on. All day there was thunder and lighting and the kids were scared. By the time dad got home things were quieting down the wind was nice and the sky was lighter. So we ate, took care of chores and went to bed. At around 3:00 I woke to a sound at the window, it was rain. Slow at first then a little harder. I prayed God would let it rain like this for days, we needed a nice and slow rain to seep into the ground the animals loved the rain they went out and play in it as soon as we would let them. We were luck it did rain off and on for ten days, sometimes heavy and sometime slow. The ponds were filling and our small creek was running again so I knew there was rain in the mountains that was good. By the end of July the grass was green, trees had fruit and would be ready to pick by fall. The animals were fat and healthy.

Since the boys each had a pony I told Rose and June they could ride Honey. I was getting a little too big for her, but I was still there with apples and carrots for her. Dad did say he was looking for two more ponies for the girls, but this way they would learn to ride on a quiet pony first. August was market month so we will have to look around. One day dad came home from work and told us that the sheriff was at Mr. Brown's home so he stopped to see if he could help. Mr. Brown said he was coming to the house for lunch and Mrs. Brown was sitting shelling peas, it looked like she had fallen to sleep but instead she had passed away. He would let everyone know when the funeral would be. Dad had stayed friends with them since they first moved into the small house he rented. We were sorry for him so mom made a plate of food and dad and the boys took it to him.

The funeral was Saturday we had to wait for his boys to get here. They all lived out of state and it took some time for all to get here. We helped clean the small house and set up beds for as many as we could, plus the farm house. Thursday, Friday and Saturday the women from church made sure there was food. The boys and their families left Sunday for home. Tuesday Mr. Brown called dad and told him he was selling the farm and he had two ponies that he wanted to give to girls if dad would take them. We are going to look at them Saturday. They were nice ponies so dad said he would pay for them, Mr. Brown said no just be sure to take good care of them. He also gave me a horse a nice gray mare, he said that was for all the help I did getting things ready for his family. I thanked him and gave him a hug. It made him cry. About two weeks later Mr. Brown pulled into our farm but went to see Matt. They talked for about a half hour then shook hands and he left. When we had dinner Matt told us he had just bought the Brown's farm, livestock and all. He was planning to start living there when Mr. Brown moved to Florida with his sister. That would be in September, he said the boys didn't want anything from the farm and so if mom or I would like to help clean things out we could have what we wanted. He was going to fix up the small house and rent it out for a little extra money. Then he will ask Cattie Lynn to marry him next spring. Mr. Anderson said he still had land for the boys to build on, Lee, Stu, Hank, Carl and Tom had all built there already and Matt was still going to be on the same road that made his mom happy.

Chapter 20

SCHOOL WAS GETTING READY TO start in two weeks, all of us will be in school this year. I was going to be a junior and the twins in first grade, boy what a span that was. Mom will have kids in school forever. Dad came home with a lot of papers for me to fill out for the grant I had some that had to be filled out by the school and copies of my grades for the last two years. I was doing the best I could, dad didn't push me but did help me when I asked. He had four kids that still needed help.

Some of the girls at school were trying to get me to join the cheerleaders they were to practice three nights a week and the games were on Fridays and some were out of town on Saturdays. I didn't want to do it I heard that some of the guys and girls were getting into trouble and a few were expelled for a few days, I was going to college and didn't need that. The older you get the harder things get. I was doing okay in school. It was hard to pick the right friends. Some had cars and wanted to go places after school and I had to get home for chores. Willis said he would help me with mine if I would let him know but that wasn't right, and mom would know if I didn't get home on time.

Then there were parties. I had a date and we went to Barry's farm for hot dogs and dancing in the barn. His folks were very nice and after we ate they went into the house. That was when the liquor came out. Some of the boys had beer and whiskey and they were trying to get some of us girls to drink Carol, Betty and I said no but my date and Carols were drinking a lot and getting mean. George even slapped Betty. With that we went to stand outside till she stopped crying. I told them I was walking home and if they wanted to come with fine, but I wasn't staying. We knew where we were at and I knew were the Stuller's house was, so we started to walk. I was worried that if the boys found out we left they would come looking for us so we watched out for cars, and if we saw one coming we went behind some trees. Yes we saw George's car and then Tom's car. They were all over the road, soon they headed back to Barry's. As soon as we saw a house I went to the door and told them what had happened and they called my folks and the police. As soon as dad got there we took Carol and Betty home.

Monday at school a lot of kids were missing. The teachers told the rest of us that we were lucky not to have gone to the party, some kids were still in jail. Dad told me that when they came back if we had any trouble with any of them then to let him know. Things were fine at school, but at home things were happening that scared the twins. The fences that keep the sheep and cows separate was cut, the chickens were let out of their coop. Matt and Willis had had it and soon were keeping all night watches. One night Willis was in the barn when He saw a match by the hay someone was going up the ladder when they got to the top Willis turned on the flood lights and started doing some work. He also put in a call to dad and Matt. Since it was one in the morning dad called the police too. As soon as the police arrived they told whoever is in the loft to come down now. Down came Barry, Lee, Tom, George and Sam. All five were taken to jail and dad pressed charges. When the police checked the loft they found two gas cans and matches. All I could think about was the animals, they were going to kill them. I told mom no more dates. Carol and Betty lived in town but their dad's cars had windows broken or tires flat.

I was glad to see Christmas in a few weeks. I would be working at dad's office for two weeks that we will be off school. I would be able to see how it is to be an accountant they would be getting ready for tax season. Monday I worked with Mrs. Brooks, she sat at the front and took calls and talked with the customers. She was a big help to the firm and I told dad so. Tuesday she had me on the phone making appointment for farmers and businesses to start getting their taxes done. Some would need to have the whole day and some would have to come back. By the end of the week I was helping the accountants lining up their paper work. Two days before Christmas I went to the store with dad and picked out some things for the men at work, I told him I had the ladies taken care of at home. I told mom I was going to give the ladies some of the things I made for weddings. No one had homemade gifts on their wedding lists so I would use them now. There were only three ladies and I know what they would like. Christmas Eve we had a party, the men like the cigars and pipe tobacco I gave them. Then the ladies opened theirs, the napkins and place mats for Mrs. Brooks were just wonderful, Mrs. Polk loved the table runner and dollies and Mrs. Watson loved her table runner and dollies too. I received a bracelet, scarf, gloves and a bonus from the boss. We had Friday, Saturday and Sunday off, then back on Monday. We worked till Thursday then off for the New Year. Mr. Copper called me into his office just before we clocked out on the 4th of January 1938, he said he was happy with my work and would like to know if this summer I would like to work here to make money for college. I was so glad, yes I would love too. I would start the second week we were out. Next year I will learn about the grant. This summer I was hoping to learn a lot from everyone at the office. I have also filled out for government grants but no answers yet.

That birthday I was 17 and had one year of school left. I was asked by Kurt Williams to the Prom. He was a senior and I was a junior. I asked mom and dad and it was ok with them. Two weeks before the prom mom and I went looking for a dress. I had a hard time finding the right color or size. I didn't like the styles so we went home with no dress. I had a lot of pictures of the ones I liked but not the right one. After dinner mom and I sat at the table going over the pictures, what about this one? Not in my color. This one not my size, and so on. Then we put all the pictures in a roll, then one at a time we would say yes or no. If no off the table. At last we were down to two. Still wrong color or size but we knew what I was looking for. Mom picked me up after school on Monday and we went to the fabric store. We found a pattern that was close but not like it. We got it anyway and I did find the color I wanted, I get a few extra yards and we went home. We had twelve days to make the dress. After dinner we would cut and pin pieces then while we were in school mom would sew what we did the night before, and soon I had something to try on. It was starting to look like the dress I wanted. I was so happy mom and I were working together for this dress. The day before the prom it was done, all the layers were just right when I tried it on we both cried. I told mom if I get married we were going to make my dress, and she said great.

The night of the prom Kurt picked me up early so we could go to have pictures at his house and dinner before the dance. We had the pictures at my house, then his. His mom and dad were really nice. We went to the Pikes Steak House for dinner. It was great. I had a wonderful time at the dance it was so beautiful pretty lights and a real band the seniors did a great job this year. I get home around 11:00 and Kurt walked me to the door. He was holding my hand and asked if he could kiss me goodnight, I said yes. I went in and mom was having coffee, I asked her to help me out of my dress and then I would tell her all about the prom. I went into the sewing room and changed. I had coffee with her and told her everything. We talked till two in the morning, I didn't have school the next day so I could sleep. School would be out soon and Kurt asked me out twice, I told him I was going to be started work soon and would only be able to go out on the week-ends. Well he was going to college in the fall and didn't want to leave a girl at home, when there would be so many new ones to meet. I told him I wished him well and good luck at school.

Chapter 21

*F*RIDAY, LAST DAY OF SCHOOL for the summer. Some sad times saying goodbye to friends that won't be back in the fall. Everyone was signing our year books and wishing everyone a fun summer. I will be starting my job on Monday and know it will be fun. I stayed around school till 3 talking to teachers and planning for the next year classes. I will be taking two college classes and still want to work. If I don't get the Grants I will still have the money to go to college, just not the one I want. It will be a long summer but I'll make it. I talked to dad on the way home, he told me he was proud of me and how I was planning ahead. I can't wait till Monday.

Mr. Copper called me into his office Monday morning to tell me I would be answering the phones for the next two weeks while Carol was on vacation, then working with Dan to learn about corporation taxes they have to file two to four times a year. The first two weeks went fast. I talked to a lot of people and made appointments for the other agents. Some people stayed with the same agent for a long time because they knew their cases. Dad had a few that asked for him. Quite a few still liked to talk with Mr. Copper. When Ms. Carol came back I started working with Dan. I learned there is a lot more to corporate taxes than personal taxes. Dan had me working on one account by myself, but he had to check all my work. I made mistakes but was a fast learner. I asked dad one night if he did corporate taxes and he said no that wasn't his department. Plus he liked the job he had. I worked with Dan for six weeks then went to Richard. He was in the same department but had a different way of doing to same thing.

Thursday when dad and I arrived home mom said I had two letters in my room. I went to read them. One letter was from Georgia State saying I was accepted to Georgia State and would I please call and make an appointment to come up and meet with them. I ran down to tell mom and dad. They were both very pleased. Dad said to ask Mr. Copper if I could call from work the next day. I was so excited I had a hard time sleeping that night. Mr. Copper said yes and called dad into his office so we could make the call. Mom, dad and I will be going up to meet with the board in two weeks. Just before school starts. Emma and Frank will watch the kids. We will be staying on the campus for three days and two nights, I can't believe this is happening to me.

Wednesday August 8th. 1938 we arrived at 9:30 to the Deans office. About six other kids were there with their folks. The Dean welcomed us and gave us papers to fill out and a guide to take us to our rooms. She said she would be back at 12:30 to take us to lunch and answer any questions we may have. While mom unpacked dad and I went over the papers. We answered all the questions and we were ready when our guide came back. Her name was Mary and she would be the one to help us through our stay. We were taken to the teachers' lounge for lunch while Mary took my papers to the Dean. Then Mary took us around the campus. By 4:30 she said we could go back to the lounge or if we wanted we could go into town for dinner. Just remember we had to be back by 9 because the gates were locked at that time. We stayed with her.

Thursday breakfast at 7:30 then to the auditorium were the Dean talked to about 350 students and parents about the school and the classes that would be given. How important it was for a clear mind and a good education. By choosing Georgia State we were off to a good start. We had more tours and questions. Then we had to talk with a counselor about what I wanted to learn and why. At 2:00 the students had tests to take while the parents went to a lawn party with the Dean and the faculty. Testing was over at 4 and Mary took me to my parents. Dad said at the lawn party the parents were giving a packet that had applications for student loans and grants. We were to look them over when we got home and try for as many as we could. We had dinner in the main hall with the Dean, his family the faculty and their families. By the time we went to bed I was so tired I fall right to sleep.

Friday morning mom was all packed dad had the car loaded and we went to have our last meal with Mary back in the main hall. After we ate the Dean wished us all a safe trip home and said he hoped to see most of us back next year. We left around 12 and headed home. Dad said we would be home around 9:00 so we better plan on stopping for dinner by 6. Mom and I did a lot of talking and I was happy to hear that she was ok with me going that far from home and having to stay there. Dad just keep saying we have to wait and see about the grants. I told him I would just pray on it and see what God had in mind for me. So happy to see the farmhouse coming upon us. We went to bed after Emma and Frank left, but first we had to tell them all about the trip. Dad told Frank you better start saving now if you're going to send yours to college. Saturday and Sunday we went over the papers and tried to figure out what to do. Dad said that Mr. Copper would know more about these things and we could ask him in the morning.

Dad gave the papers to Mr. Copper the next day and he said he would look them over then talk with us. All day the people in the office were asking us about what happened in Georgia. After lunch Mr. Copper called us to his office. He said he checked out the list and marked the ones that he would choose for his daughter if he had one. Plus he would let me know in January about the grant from his group. I did thank him for his help and told him I would be starting school in three weeks. I would like to work after school again this year to help save money. He was pleased to hear that.

Chapter 22

SEPTEMBER 7ᵀᴴ, 1938 FIRST DAY of school. Dad dropped me off and I told him I would walk to the office as soon as I got out. I had a lot of homework and so many books that I didn't know if I could go to school and work. I will have to try it for a few weeks and see how it goes.

Sunday I would have to thank dad and Sammy for all their help and to watch over Honey for me. The next two week things got better. I was doing well in school and learning a lot from Richard and Dan. If I had a problem I could ask, and they would show me how to work it out. Dad and I will start sending out the letters to the companies that had the grants for next year and for student loans. All we could do now is wait. I met a few guys in school and did go out a few times but not a lot. I needed to think about my life and where it was going. Most of the kids were into partying and drinking and that was not my thing, so I stayed home a lot. Then one day a new boy stated at our school. His dad bought the hardware store. He worked there after school and had a car. We would talk at lunch about our jobs and things we had to give up. He was planning to go to college to be a doctor, so he didn't go out much either. So we started to date, went to the movies a few times and to school dances. The hardware store was closed on Sundays so he would come out to the farm. Dale and I were going to help the church set up a Halloween party for the kids. Dad said we could have it here at the farm, the parents could come with the kids and bring their treats so the kids would not have to go out on the streets. We had games and prizes, soda and popcorn plus snacks for everyone. By 9:30 it was over and all went home. We all had a great time, dad and the kids helped us clean up the barn and then we had homemade ice cream.

Sunday after church I went to talk to dad. I told him all about Dale and how nice he was and that I was glad he had his head on straight and was going to take me to homecoming dance next week. I was so glad to have a friend like him.

We went to the dance after pictures and dinner, had a good time till around 8:30, Dale keep going over by a few of the guys that I didn't run with. When he came over for a dance I could smell beer on him so I asked him about it. He said one of the guys spilled some on him but he was fine. I said okay when the dance was over I went to the ladies room and some of the girls were there one was crying and her dress was torn. I asked what happened and Sally said Katie was outside with Ray and he tried to get fresh and tore Katie's dress. He was drinking beer. He never acted like this before. I went to find Dale and tell him what happened, when I went outside I saw him drinking a beer with the guys. I went back inside and called my dad. I told the girls that my dad was on his way and anyone that wanted a ride home we would take them. Katie and four others said okay.

Dad took them home and helped Katie into the house. Someone called the police and the school closed the dance just before they got there. At 12:30 Dale called and dad talked to him, I was in bed. Dad said it sounded like he was at a party somewhere. I was so glad I called dad. Monday at school I heard that three cars were drag racing and that there was an accident three boys and a girl were killed and five were in the hospital. By noon the principle came on the speaker and told us about the accident. Ray Collins, George Pile, Michael Herald and Sally Green were killed. I almost passed out, not Sally. He named the ones in the hospital but I didn't know them. Then he asked if anyone knew were the beer came from, no one said a word but you could hear a lot of crying. School was let out for the rest of the day. As I was leaving school Dale came up to me and said he was sorry and it won't happen again. I told him I hope not because if he wants to go to college he would have to walk the line. He asked if I would go the movies this Saturday and I said no. Then I went to work, dad came over to me when I walked in and put his arms around me and I cried. I asked Mr. Copper if he could take me home so we left. Thursday I went to Sally's funeral it was so hard on her parents. She was their only child. All of November was a long month, I still saw Dale at school and he was now running with the wrong guys. I pray for him but I can't stop him.

Chapter 23

ECEMBER STARTED OUT COLD. BETWEEN work and school I was kept busy. Mom and I still made things for the tree and the girls would show me what they were making for mom and dad. I helped them wrap their things and set them under the tree. Yes we still made things for the family and some friends. Not like we did when I was young, but we still had fun. We saw my Uncle's at church with their families. So many of their kids were married and now they had grandkids. Still one big happy family. Christmas break I shopped for the people at work, we will be having our party the Friday before Christmas. We had a lot of food and fun. Everyone liked the things they got then Mr. Copper passed out his gift cards to everyone. Inside my card was a letter telling me that I was getting the grant from his group of investors it would pay for my books and room and board for two years. I ran to dad and showed him. Also in the card was a check for $1,000.00 to help with clothes and school supplies. I couldn't wait to tell mom. Next I went over to Mr. Copper and gave him a big hug and kiss on the cheek. He just smiled and said Merry Christmas and do them all proud. Mom was just as surprised as I was. Tomorrow go put the check in the bank and we will look at the papers they gave us from the school. School was out and work was closed till January 3rd 1939.

Christmas Day the kids were up at 5:30 but mom made them wait till the boys were in for breakfast before the gifts. Matt and Willis came in with more gifts, after breakfast they would be going home for the day. As soon as we were done we went into the frontroom and dad put on the tree lights. The boys were happy with the things the girls made for them and thanked everyone, Dad then pass out the rest of the things and the boys left. Toys and games. New clothes and boots. Everyone had more scarfs then the winter was long, but we told them how nice they were. It was hard to believe the year was almost over. In a week it will be 1938 and what will that bring. Since it was a nice day dad and the kids went out to play in the snow. Yelling and screaming, snowballs flying they were having fun. As mom and I cleaned up the kitchen she ask me if I remembered playing like that, yes I'm so glad that she married Larry and gave me my family now to enjoy. She hugged me then I went to study.

On New Year's Eve, we went to church and I talked to dad and Sammy, a new year will be here soon and I still miss you dad. I know Larry has been so good to me and loves me as much as the others, but sometimes I wonder what it would be like if you were still here. Well it is starting to snow so we need to leave, I'll talk to you and Sammy soon. Happy New Year. That night we had our soda and popcorn, cookies and snacks. We watched the fireworks from the front porch, hit the pans and yelled Happy New Year. I think the only ones that heard us were the animals. It was fun. Now hot chocolate and off to bed, four very tired little kids.

So glad to be back in school and work. I had to send the college a copy of my grant and that I was still waiting about the others I applied for. Things were going along fine. Spring was just around the corner and I would be able to work full time for a week. This was a very busy time for us. Sometimes dad would have to work over and I would do what I could. Taxes were due in three weeks and people were waiting for the last minute to get them done.

I was able to get them started with their taxes then one of the others would take over. We didn't have a bad winter it was just so many things happened to so many people. I was glad to see the 15th of April come, there were a few that were still late but they were done for the year. Mr. Copper was a very happy man. He told everyone that he was thinking of putting two people on the payroll for this time next year. Of course Sara you will still have a job here when you come home on breaks, so don't worry. I told him thank you that I would let him know when they would be. Easter the church had an Easter egg hunt for the kids, they had a ball. Mom would have to make a lot of egg salad and still have some left over.

Back to school tomorrow. Mom is worried about the twins. They have had sore throats and the doctor said they had Scarlet Fever. They each had a fever of 102.5 they were sent to the hospital. Dad was to bring all of us to the doctor's office so we could be checked out. Mom was going to stay there and dad and I were to go and check the boys. No fevers, so far so good. The next morning we sat at the office and waited our turn to see the doctor. Dad asked about the girls and was told they were the same. Then we were all checked and given a shot. The doctor said he had two more cases in the hospital. The county closed the school for a week to see if more broke out. The county sent out doctors and nurses to the homes with kids in our schools and everyone was given a shot. Even Matt and Willis were given shots.

The only place the twins were around other kids was at church and the two that were in the hospital went to our church. Before the week was over there were eight more cases. Not as bad as the twins because they had the shot. The church was closed till the ladies could clean the class rooms. I went and helped. Mom called dad and said Rose was getting better, but June was up 103.7 and they put Rose in another room. The nurses were giving June cold baths to bring the fever down, so far it didn't work. I went to sit with Rose, mom stayed with June and dad was back and forth. By the end of week two Rose was up and playing. The doctor said if no fever she could go home tomorrow after he saw her. June was losing weight, but doing a little better. Her fever was down to 101.9 but she still slept most of the time. Dad made mom go home and get some rest before she got sick herself and the doctor told her to stay home for two days unless he called her. Dad and I stayed with June. I called mom every time the doctors saw her and if things changed. After two and a half days June started to move and cry out in her sleep. The doctor said to call mom to come back. The fever had done something to her brain and she was having a bad time. Dad, mom and I sat around her bed with the hospital pastor praying for her. At 3:48 am on May 23rd. 1939 June passed away. Poor mom she broke up pretty bad. Dad did the best he could to help her. I told them I would call the families. I told my uncles then called Emma and Frank. I told them we would be home soon not to tell the kids. Mom and dad would.

We buried June next to Sammy on MAY 27, 1939. It was so hard trying to watch this happen. We were going to get a tombstone of an angel with her name. I told Dad and Sammy that I prayed they would watch over her, that she was special to all of us. Aunt Kate helped out around the house for a few days, mom was feeling better and so she went home. The county found out that Mr. and Mrs. Patterson's Grandkids that were here for the holidays had it and that was what started it in church. There were cases at the school in Kentucky were they lived but didn't know that till they returned home. Because they lived back in the hills no one knew what was wrong till it was too late. They lost seven kids, and had twelve in the hospital. At church we prayed for all of them. The school opened and dad went back to work. I had to go back to school so Emma came over in the morning to help mom, they would start working on small blankets for the hospital children's ward. They needed plenty so we all helped with them. Soon mom was almost her old self again that made all of us feel better. We won't forget June, but she is with God and playing with all the little kids in heaven.

Chapter

24

Before you knew it school was out for the summer, I would graduate and work at the office till school started in the fall. I received two more grants so all my schooling was taken care of. I had the money to pay for the things they didn't and I would still work for Mr. Copper on breaks and over the summer. I only had two years to become an accountant, but if I wanted to get a BD I could go for two more years. I wanted to wait and see how this went first. The rest of the school year went fast. The day of Graduation was bright and sunny. I had my cap and gown, mom helped me pick out a nice dress and shoes to match. Mr. and Mrs. Anderson sat by mom and dad, they had a boy in class too. Also all my uncles and aunts were there. Mr. & Mrs. Copper were there too. When my name was called I was so proud to walk up and get my diploma, mom was crying and dad was yelling. The kids and the rest of the families were clapping. After we got home we had a large party. Food, cake and gifts. Besides money I got school supplies and some clothes. We had a great time. I told Mr. Copper I would be back to work on Monday, but he gave me a week off. I would have to leave for school September the 3rd so I needed to spend some time with my mom. Dad told us that Mr. Copper hired two new men, one was 35 and just moved to town and the other still had one more year of school. I would be helping them learn the way we do things at our branch starting next week. That was great.

I met George first, he was the older one, I took him were his desk would be and since he met the rest of the people Saturday I gave him the accounts that Mr. Copper said to start him on. Anthony was the one still in school, he was two years older than me and was happy to have a job.

He needed to work to go back to school in the fall, he was working on his B D and still had I year to go. By the second week they both were doing a good job. I told them this was the slow time of the year, wait till after the first of the year. After a few weeks Anthony asked me out. We went to the movies and had a lot of fun. He said that Mr. Copper was him great uncle and his mom helped get him this job for the summer. But he wasn't sure he would stay in this small town when he was out of school. I told him he had a year and a half to think about it. That he had to pray to God for the answer. I worked all summer and Anthony and I went out every weekend. By the middle of August Anthony had to leave and go back home he went to collage there in his home town. We said we would write and see each other on breaks. We had a going away party at the office with cake and ice cream. I told him I only had a week left to work then get ready for mom and dad to take me off to school. The last week Mr. Copper asked if I would have dinner with him and his wife on Saturday at his home. I said yes I would be happy too. I told him I didn't drive so dad would have to bring me, he said no I will send my car for you at 4:30, and we eat at 5:00.

I was picked up at 4:30 sharp and was at their home at 4:40. I met Mrs. Copper at the door. We had a lovely dinner, a nice Roast, Mrs. Copper asked me about the school I was going to and would I miss my family very much? I knew this was a new venture but I needed to do this, so I could better myself and make my family proud of me. I would be home on breaks and for the summer. I will still see her at the company picnic in the summer. After dinner we sat in the frontroom and had coffee. Mr. Copper told me he was proud of my work and would be glad to have me work full time for him when I was done with school. He would always have a place for me in his office. Then they gave me a personal check for $1,000.00 and told me if things got hard for me and if I needed more money to let them know. I was like a daughter to them and I made them feel good helping me and my family. They asked if I would write to them a least once a month and let them know what was happening. At 8:30 I was taken home. I had to tell mom and dad about my visit, and showed them the check. Dad said to put it in the bank until you need it. I signed the check and dad would put it in the bank Monday, I would be home with mom getting my things ready to leave on Friday. Anthony called to tell me he missed me. He was trying to get a transfer to the school I would be going to, he had an aunt that lived in the same town and he would stay there. He would be able to pay for his classes from the money he made this summer. I told him that would be nice. I hope he can do it. I was sure that if he took time he would meet a few girls there that he would like to hang around with. Only time will tell. I spent the time with the kids, they all know how to ride and each had their own ponies. We went out for a ride twice that week. Dad called me it was time to go.

Chapter 25

THE RIDE WAS NICE AND when we stopped for dinner, we had the talk about if I needed them I was to call and they would come for me. After we ate we went to bed so we could be at the school by 9:00 that was when we would find out what dorm I would be in. Dad would help me take my things up and mom would help me unpack before they left. I met three of the girls I would be rooming with, and the floor mother. They were all very nice, I was sure things would work out. We went to supper and then they left. I stood in the parking lot and for the first time I cried. Then I looked up to heaven and knew that Dad, Sammy and June were there with me and I would be fine. I was not alone. I was 18 and had two years to prove myself. I checked my classes and Jane, Carol and I were in the same rooms so we would be able to find everything together. Mary was taking other classes so we would only see her in our room and on weekends. Monday morning we made it to our first class in time. Each class was an hour long. Each of our Professors were nice, they said we would start slow and build ourselves up to a faster pace. By the time we were back in our room we had four hours of homework. Mary told us to get used to it, it will only get worse. So this was collage. By Saturday we had books everywhere. I got a letter from Anthony, he would have to wait till next semester to change schools. So he stayed where he was for now. The first few weeks we more or less stayed in our room studying, it helped that we all had the same work we could help each other and that was better. I wrote mom and Anthony telling them what was going on. In October football games would start and we would go together and cheer them on. All four of us went to church on Sunday so that made mom happy. Told mom I would be home Wednesday to Sunday for Thanksgiving and I would be taking the train it would take me six hours and I would be in Jamestown at 12 noon. I would have to leave Sunday at 6:45p.m. To get back to school before 1:30a.m. To get the school bus that is waiting for us. That was nine weeks away. School was doing fine, tell dad I sure have to study harder here. A lot of what I'm learning is like they do at the office. So I can help the girls. There are somethings I have to work hard to learn but I will do it. This was sure something new and we had to make the best of it.

Sunday after church we walked around town and had lunch, we had three hours before the last bus left for the campus so it was time for some time off. At the restaurant Mary met two guys from one of her classes so we joined them. They were nice we talked about school and what we were studying. Tom and Glen said they had a car if we wanted to go back with them. Mary said yes but we said we were going on the bus, and we did. Mary went with them. When she got back it was late. She told us they helped her meet half of the football team. They were all at the main hall watching some football game on television. I'll wait till our school has games to meet them. Carol was having a hard time with her studies she was having trouble remembering what we just did. She also was tripping a lot. Our Professors tried not to notice but sometimes she would start talking about something unknown to any of us. After our last class that Monday Jane and I took her to the nurse. We told her what was going on and that she needed help. The school sent her to the hospital for tests, her parents were called. We didn't hear anything till we came in from class and all her things were gone. Our floor mother Meg said her folks came for her things, Carol had Polio and had to go to a hospital back home. Anything left we should keep if we wanted.

I sat and wrote to mom about it, we were all upset. Mary, Jane and I had to have blood tests but we were fine. Our room was so quiet without her. As the days passed we got back to our studies. The school's first game is this week, Our Bulldogs will be playing the Ravens. It has been cold and raining all week, so many kids have been sick, I don't know if Jane and I will go to the game. Wednesday it was raining hard when we headed to our first class, after the second period classes were cancelled for the rest of the day. We were asked to check in with our floor mothers that we were in for a bad weekend. Also the game was cancelled too, some roads were flooded and the river was up to the banks. Our school was high on a hill but the low lands could be in trouble if it keep raining.

By Friday the police were asking if the older boys would help fill sand bags. The river banks were over flowing and houses were flooding. Older girls asked to help but were told no the water was running to fast. Saturday and Sunday it kept coming down. Parents were calling from all over my folks too. Monday as we woke it was so quiet, did it stop? Yes the sun was out, Praise God. Still no school, Professors had to wait till the roads were safe to drive on. Tuesday morning a bus brought the boys back, the school had a luncheon in their honor. Wednesday some classes will start up again, Jane and I had two of them so back to studying. We did keep up with our reading and asking each other questions when the lights were on.

I had seven letters going out, I was surprised I haven't heard from Anthony in the last two weeks. Must be because of the rain. Five weeks till Thanksgiving, I can't wait to get home. I love school but miss my family and friends. Jane told me she lived about twenty miles from Carol's and would try seeing her if she had time. We have been sending cards and letters to her. Her mom would send little notes back so we were keeping in touch. Today we had mail, I read the ones from home and the Copper's first then Anthony's. He was sorry about the floods and the few lives that were lost. He knew that I would be brave and strong. Then he said he was going to stay in school where he was. He had made some friends and was having a good time, he hoped I didn't mind. He was sure I must have met some guy myself so I would understand. His girlfriend's name was Sandy and she was great. I'm happy for him, sure I won't be hearing much more from him. The next few weeks flew by it was time to pack for home. Mary was leaving Tuesday but Jane and I had to wait till Wednesday morning. We sat up most of the night talking. After breakfast we sat out for the buses to town. We will meet at the station on Sunday evening.

When my train pulled in to town all my family was waiting for me. Mom and dad let the kids come running to me first for all the hugs and kisses. Dad told me I had grown so much in the last few months, mom just hugged me and cried. Everyone started talking as soon as we were in the car. Thursday we would have Thanksgiving at home just our family. Friday I was to have dinner with the Copper's, Saturday all my uncles and aunts were meeting at the church for lunch. I'm so glad I didn't have plans. This would be a full week-end and a lot of fun.

It was nice to be home, mom did a lot of baking she said there was a package for me to take back for the girls. She made a roast for dinner and as I was setting the table. We had a nice talk. She asked if I met any nice boys at school, I told her no I'm not looking. I want to study and pass this year, school comes first right now. I told her Anthony was staying at his school he met a nice girl and was sorry if he hurt me. I'm glad he is staying. We called the family to dinner and had to tell the kids all about the rain storm.

Friday I went to the Copper's. I was met at the door, Mrs. Copper was like a mother, and Mr. Copper asked all the questions. We sat in the frontroom while we talked. I asked to help put out the food but was told I needed to talk to Mr. Copper. We went to the den and talked, first about Spring Break, was I coming home or going somewhere with friends? Told him I was coming home. It was a two week break and I would like to work if he would have me. Mr. Copper said of course if you want, but if you need money to go with your friends He would give it to me. No I want to come home I miss everyone here so much. Next about school, did I need anything like money or clothes? No I have everything I need. Then he asked if it would be okay if he and Mrs. Copper came up some week-end? Yes, that would be great. Mrs. Copper called us to dinner. Mrs. Copper said she would let me know when they would be up. Soon it was time to leave and their driver took me home.

Sunday after dinner dad helped me to the train station, mom packed a snack for me and four boxes of bake goods to share with the girls. Dad laughed you know she wants to bring up more food for you to share. Dad, I will be home for Christmas in thirty two days so just ask her to wait till next year. I asked what the kids wanted for Christmas, I will try and pick up somethings then get the rest when I get home. I gave him a big hug as I boarded the train. Soon we were on our way and I leaned back to get some rest. It had been a busy five days. The girls will be glad to see me back.

Chapter

26

*T*HIS MONTH WAS SO BUSY, we had tests for two weeks straight. Plus I had shopping for gifts for my friends and family. I got a call from Mrs. Copper that they were coming up two days before school was out and would stay to bring me home. That way if I had things to bring home there would be room. After class one day as I opened my door I heard Jane crying. She looked up and said, my parents said I can't come home for Christmas. They're getting a divorce and dad was going to be with his girlfriend and mom was going to New York to see her sister. Aunt Sally didn't have room for her and she didn't like Jane anyway. She would have to stay at the school for Christmas break. Her folks would send her money so she could get what she wanted. I felt so sorry for her. We had two weeks to go. I had a lot of study hall work to do, we were going to have tests the week before break. I talked to mom and Mr. Cooper, both said yes to Jane coming home with me for break. Mrs. Copper wanted to ask her, so I had to wait till they get there. Mary left for home Monday and the Copper's will be here Wednesday we were moving right along. They called at one to ask us out for dinner. It was lots of fun. Mr. Copper had Jane laughing so much. All in all it was a great night. We only had a half day of classes so we would be picked up at noon for some shopping. It was just us girls and the driver. What a long day. We had lunch and shopped for hours. Jane and Mrs. Copper shopped for the ladies from work and her friends. Jane got a few gifts too. I was glad we had a car to go home to fit everything we bought. At dinner that night Mrs. Copper asked Jane if she would like to come home with us for Christmas break. If so we will be leaving at two the next day. That night she asked me if I would mind if she went with us, no that would be great. We would see each other over break.

So at 1:45 they were there for us. We pack the car with Pete's help and got on the road. We had a great time Mr. Copper asked all about school, told Jane that I was going to work for him through break, but would like for her to come to the office and help if she wanted. We stopped for the night and dinner. Jane and I had our own room. Pete joined us for dinner he had more story's and jokes to tell. At bed that night we were like two kids at a sleep over. Finally we fell asleep. At six we had our wake up call, breakfast was at seven. Then we got on the road, we were home by four o'clock. My family was so happy to see us, there was a snow storm coming in that night or tomorrow morning. I got my things from the car. Then they were on their way home. The next day was Christmas Eve. Mom and we girls did a lot of baking and cooking, The Copper's and Jane were coming here tomorrow for the day. Frank and his family would be here too. We had to be up by six to have breakfast ready by the time everyone got here. Soon there was noise everywhere. Dad had tables set up and the boys set up the chairs. Mom's made the kids plates first, then the older ones made theirs. Dad said grace and soon everyone was eating. By Ten o'clock it was time for gifts. The kids were first then the rest. Mr. And Mrs. Copper gave everyone a gift, so did Frank and Emma. Mom and dad gave me a new winter coat and boots. The Copper's gave Jane and me sweaters and bracelets. Frank and Emma gave gloves and scarfs. All and all we all had a good time. After cleaning up we helped in the kitchen, soon Jane and I were sent out of the room. We went to the room I shared with the girls. We spent a few hours looking over my things I saved over the years, then went to see the ponies. Soon we were called to dinner, dad said grace and we all ate so much that we needed a nap before cake and pie. The kids took their friends to their rooms, men in the frontroom Jane and I in the sewing room and the ladies in the kitchen. I showed Jane some of the things mom and I made for my tree when I get married. That started us talking about boys and I would stand up for her and she mine. About six o'clock we were called for desert. The cake was so moist and the frosting creamy. Mom's pies had juice running out of them. After we were done, Jane and I sent all the ladies to the frontroom and we cleaned up. Soon it was time for all to leave. I had two days till work and I wanted to spend time with mom. If Jane wanted to come over she could or if she wanted to help Mrs. Copper she could it was her vacation too. The Copper's were having New Year's Eve at their house for everyone that was at Christmas.

The next two days mom and I did a lot of talking about school, if I was going to work for Mr. Copper after I graduated. Was I going to get a place of my own in town? Not that she didn't want me home but I was getting older and they could get to me in a few minutes if I needed them. If I wanted a place of my own, dad would start looking in next April for a nice apartment for me and they would start getting some furniture from the families like we all did to help the other kids. I told her I would have to think about it for a while. We did some shopping for school and I got the kids a few things they could use in school.

New Year's Eve, we had fireworks and lots of food. The Copper's gave everyone a gift, the boys all got a little car and the girls a doll. Each adult a small bag of chocolate coins. Each gift had a note with it. We had to read the note and say what it meant to you. Mine was where would you like to be in five years? I said I would be out of school and working at a good job, and maybe going to night school. Jane's was where do you want to live when you get married? She said in a small town like ours just depends where her husband wanted. Dad's was, do you like your job and why? Yes I love my job, there is room to grow and everyone is so nice to work with. Mom's was, where would you like to see yourself in the next ten years? She said she would like to be sitting on her swing with a grandbaby or two to play with. Frank was asked how many children he would want. He said three, 3 boys was plenty. Emma laughed hers asked if she wanted to find a job. No she said she had two, one at school and one at home. Soon it was time to send the tired kids home. 1939 was gone and 1940 was here. Mr. Copper asked me to stay a while and he would bring me home. I helped mom and dad get the kids into the car and told them I would be home soon. I had to start packing for the trip back to school in four days.

As we sat in the frontroom drinking tea and had cookies, Mr. Copper asked Jane and me if we would like for my dad to drive us back to school. Then we could spend time with him, He would give my dad a paid vacation. I don't know if all the things we have would fit in dad's car but I would ask him? Mr. Copper said he would do that for me, now Sara I know you want to start working for me when you come home after you graduate. Jane is thinking of coming back and working here till she knows what she wants. I told them about what mom and I talked about me finding a place to stay in town and if Jane was coming back that would work out fine. We could rent a place together. But we still had a year and a half to go. After more talk he got the car to take me home. On the road he said the April before Graduation he and dad would have a few places for us to look at, he said that a friend at the bank was telling him about a few homes that were going to be up for rent, that we would pay the rent at the bank he would look into it for us. Jane and I would have time to think and talk about it at school and he would call us a week before we are to come home. I was so tired when I got home it was 3 am and I wanted to sleep so I went right to bed.

When I got up Rose came running upstairs to tell me the vet was here, I threw on my jeans and shirt and went downstairs for my boots and jacket. On the way to the barn Rose asked me if I was going to let Honey have a baby again, I said no, why? Because the vet is checking her like she is. I hurried to the barn and to Honey. Is she ok I asked the vet? Well she is fine but has a little trouble with her bowels you know she is getting older. I will send your mom medicine for her to have once a day it will help but not fix anything, like I said she is up in years. Maybe two or three more years in her. He was done with her hooves so I took her to the other end so we could talk. I told her how much I loved her and that she was the best friend I had in the world. As I brushed her I talked about the years we spent together, about her babies and how well they were doing. I thanked her for letting everyone learn to ride on her and she was a great teacher. After the vet left mom came to me and asked why I was crying, told her I didn't realize I was. Well she was going to start dinner dad would be home from work soon. I put Honey back in her stall and went to help mom.

At dinner I looked around the table and for the first time really looked at the kids, the boys were now fifteen and thirteen they had all grown so much in the last few years, doing well in school and all helping on the farm with the chores. I miss all of that. After dinner while the kids were watching television dad, mom and I talked. Mr. Copper called him to the office and asked if he would like to take us back to school. He said no he had two clients coming in the next two weeks and they were big accounts for the company. He has been doing them for the last seven years and knew everything about their taxes. He asked me if I understood why. Of course I do. Good because Mr. Copper is leaving him in charge and will be taking us back. We leave in two days.

Chapter
27

R. AND MRS. COPPER WERE very quiet for the first few hours, finally Jane asked if something was wrong? No we are just thinking about how it will be with you girls gone. It will be fine we will be back for Spring break for two weeks. Then back for the summer, we all laughed. We had a good time the rest of the trip. At school things changed, we had a new girl in our room. She seemed like a nice girl. Her name was Barbara from New York and in her last year. When Mary came in you could tell they didn't like each other. Mary put her things away and left the room, didn't say a word to anyone. Jane and I were beside ourselves. Barbara put her things away and went to the dining room. Soon Mary was back, she told us that Barbara was a spy for her dad. If she did anything wrong he would pull her out of school and she wouldn't graduate. After school he had plans for her to marry well in the upper class and Barbara was to make sure of it. We helped Mary go through all her notes, letters, books and stories she had written. She took them over to a friend's room. After that we all stayed away from Barbara. She would start asking us things about Mary. Where she would go, and if she would date anyone? Finally Jane told her if she wanted to know ask Mary. Now our room is quiet.

January and February were long cold months. Three more weeks and spring break. Jane received a letter from her mom telling her she had to come home for Easter to call her this week-end. Jane was upset, why did she want her now? She called her mom Saturday, you could hear Jane yelling down the hall. When she came back to the room she was crying. She was to go to New York for Easter. Mom was sending a car for her. She was so unhappy. Mary, Jane and I would go for walks so we could talk. Jane asked Mary if she would like a ride to New York with her, Mary said yes be don't say a thing to Barbara. As break arrived I was getting ready for the train, and Barbara came back from lunch. Where are the girls she wanted to know? Gone some guy came and they left in his car. Who? When? Where are they going? I don't know and didn't ask. I left for the bus, it would take us to town to the train. Barbara went to town with us, she looked all over the station for the girls. When the train pulled out she was still standing there.

By Friday all the eggs were cooked and tonight the kids would color them. Saturday Dad and Rose would take ten dozen to the church for the hunt on Sunday. I went to the barn to see Honey to give her the carrots I saved for her. Helped with chores then in to help mom with the bread. Mom said Sara, Jane called and was very upset. She will try and reach you late tonight. Now what was going on? We had dinner and as soon as we had the kids in bed she called. The reason her mom and aunt wanted her in New York was a guy named Albert. He had been at her side since she got to New York. Mom and auntie were pushing them together. She could only go out if Albert took her. There was a big gala for Easter lunch, and Albert wanted to tell everyone they were getting married. She said no. Her family and his were very upset. Mom told his dad she would take care of it and when school was out there would be a wedding. She asked if she could come out to the farm for the next week. I would let the Copper's know. She will call when she gets on the train leaving New York.

Easter Sunday was a nice warm and sunny day. After church I went to talk to dad, Sammy and June. I told them how school was and soon I would be out for summer and about my friends and I told them I would be back in May, two months seem like forever, but we will make it. Jane arrived Monday and The Coppers picked her up. We talked like we haven't seen each other for months. Jane's mom only wanted Jane and Albert to get married so she would be in the upper class. She kept telling Jane if she didn't marry him she would cut Janes allowance and she would have nowhere to live. Jane didn't love or even like Albert. So after dinner we took her to the Copper's. Tuesday morning I got a call from Janes Mother, were is she? I want to talk to her right now. I told her Jane wasn't here. Well she would be here in ten hours and Jane better be ready to go back.

Albert was with her. I called Jane and told her what was going on, she would get back to me. Dad told me that Mrs. Copper and Jane were leaving for Miami in an hour and Mr. Copper was to be at work. They would be back by Saturday so we could go back to school. Wednesday we were all working and Mrs. Blake came flying in the door yelling were is Jane? Dad and Mr. Copper took her and Albert in the office. You could hear them yelling. She was going to stop paying for the school and her room and board, see how she would like that. They left and an hour later Mr. Copper's housekeeper called, they were out to the house looking for Jane the cook and housekeeper ran them off. They left town.

Saturday I took the bus to Jamestown and met Mr. and Mrs. Copper and Jane. We had lunch and left for school. When we arrived there was a note on Jane's bed. Her mother stopped payment for her schooling and for her room and board. If she changed her mind to call and things would return to normal. Mr. Copper took the letter and said don't worry go to class in the morning. There is only two and a half months then we will be out. A few hours later Mary came in but no Barbara. Daddy let her go because she lost Mary. The next two months were tough. We had so many tests we were glad Mary was there to help us. Down to the last three weeks and we were making out Mary's invitations to the graduation. There were only so many seats and so she could only have four. Jane told her mom she wasn't returning to New York. She had a job and was staying down here. She is an adult and can take care of herself. The day of graduation Mary, Jane and I sat looking at each other and crying. We would miss each other, but we would write and call. Jane and I were going to work for Mr. Copper. Mary said while she was home she met up with her boyfriend and they're going to get married and we were going to the wedding. A summer wedding in Vermont. What a great summer this is going to be. Well we had one more event and that was to watch Mary walk across the stage and receive that diploma. All of us had a great time and then said goodbye till the wedding. We packed the cars and headed home, it felt so good.

When we arrived home mom asked me to come into the bedroom, dad was there too. She said this morning the boys went to bring in the horses for the blacksmith to shoe and check their feet. Sara, they found Honey laying under the big tree on the hill. They came for mom and she called the vet, Honey is gone. The vet said her heart just gave out. I went to the hill and sat with her as the boys were digging a hole. I talked to her and said she will meet Sammy and June, they will care for her. As I sat there I make a braid from her mane for me to keep, she will always be with me. I saw them put straw in the bottom first, after she was in they would add more hay to keep her clean. I thanked them and dad took me home. I went to my room and stayed there crying till dinner.

Chapter 28

EVERYONE WAS HAPPY TO SEE us back at work. Mr. Copper has put a second story on his building. There were more offices and plus 3 more guys working. The upstairs was full and the doors had numbers and names on them. Since Jane still wasn't sure what she wanted to do with her life, she would be taking over Mrs. Brooks' job. Now that we were back, she could retire and leave Mr. Copper in good hands. Mrs. Brooks would be leaving two weeks, so Jane would have time to work with her. That would give Mr. Copper time to fine someone when we go back to school. Then Mrs. Copper and dad took me to my office, on the door was my name and # 3. It was a nice room, dad said I would start out with some of the small farmers and build up a customer's list up. This was fine with me.

We helped around the office for a week when we were called into Mr. Copper's office. He wanted to have us help Mrs. Copper with the retirement party for Mrs. Brooks. Sure we would love too.

Mrs. Copper had rented a hall in Jamestown to have the party. We had to send out invitations but try and not let on at work. Jane and I could do this in my office and Jane would take them right to the post office. The next day Mrs. Copper asked Mrs. Brooks if she and her husband would have dinner with them on Saturday night. He would sent the car for them. They didn't like to drive at night. So we were set. When we had lunch with Mrs. Brooks all we talked about was how the summer was going and what we planned on doing. Saturday night when they arrived at the restaurant everyone were sitting at the tables talking, when they were led to their table we all stood up and cheered. She was so surprised to see all of us. There were 83 people there. What a grand time we had good food and dancing and then Mr. Copper gave a toast to her for the 39 years she gave to his company. So as for a going away gift from the company he was sending them to Hawaii for two weeks, plus spending money to get things they may want. As people were leaving they would stop by her table with a gift or a card. I think that was the best day of her life.

Things were going fine at work we did our jobs, went to the movies and pretty much stayed on the farm. We had two months before back to school for our last year. Then Mary called, Eddie got cold feet and left town so the wedding was off. She said we could come up for a week or two if we had time. Told her thank you but we needed to work to help pay for school. She was sorry but then she would go to Paris with her mom. Wished her a good time, talked for a while and hung up. We were really happy for her. On the 4th of July we had a parade in town and a picnic at the park. Everyone had fun and as it started to get dark we all sat on blankets to watch the fireworks. In August Mr. Copper hired Helen for the phones, she would work with Jane for three weeks then we would be leaving for school. The Copper's took us back up to school we had dinner and stayed with them at the motel for the night. Wake up call at 6 and then we ate so they could get home before night fall. Pete is a good driver so we didn't worry.

We had a new room and new hall. Two girls were there when we arrived, twins, Kathy and Karen. But Kathy was going to learn to be a nurse, Karen wanted to work in a lab. We all received our classes so we showed the girls around campus. Karen had a car so they went into town. I told them to be back by 9:30 because they lock the gate. Jane and I were tired so we went to bed after dinner. At 11:30 the floor mother received a call from the guard at the gate asking if Kathy and Karen were her girls, yes let them in. She met them in the hall and told them if they were out after 9:30 the school would call the parents and send them home. You can bet it didn't happen again. School started out slow but started to pick up in October, football was here and we had a great team. The girls were gone most of the time. I don't know when they had time to study. One night Karen asked Jane if she would help her with a paper that was due soon. We sat down with her and she didn't know a thing that the paper was to be about. She started to cry and asked if we would do it for her. Jane said no but we will help you if you want to try. Then she left the room. Both were getting good grades so maybe they were studying with someone in their classes.

One week till Thanksgiving and then home for five days. We packed and left on the bus for the train. We would be at the farm by 2:00. Met dad at the office and I rode home with him and Jane with Mr. Copper. I told mom and dad that when we came home for Christmas we would talk about what we were going to do when we were out of school for good. Only six more months. Everyone came to moms for dinner all the kids have grown so much. The boys were as tall as dad, and Frank's boys were as tall as me. Where did the time go? Peter would be out of high school and off to college next fall. Paul one year behind him. One wanted to be a doctor and the other a vet. Rose still had three years of high school to go. Mom had pack food for us to take to school. We would be eating food for a month just in time to come home for Christmas. Told the Coppers we would let them know what day we would be out for Christmas break. If the weather was bad we would take the train home. Okay we will wait and see.

Back at school our room was dark, no one was there. I asked the floor mother were the girls were? She wasn't sure but both left school for good. Heard at lunch that a group of kids had a wild party the night before we left for Thanksgiving and the school found out about it and all the kids were expelled and would not be back. Their parents had to come and get them and their things. Well we had four weeks till Christmas and we had tests almost every day. Glad we had the room to ourselves. Mrs. Copper called they would be here on Friday to pick us up, please be ready by noon. Sure we will. Jane's mom called to see if she was coming home for Christmas, no she had a job for ten days. After all I have to pay my way through school. Then hung up on her.

Christmas was at Franks and Emma's this year. It was like we were all one big family. We were the only family the Coppers had so it was nice. Before the New Year we sat down with my folks and the Copper's to talk about when we were out of school for good. Jane and I were going to look for a place to rent so we could still work at the office. Dad said they would start looking for a place in April and start getting furniture round up from the families like we do for everyone else. Mrs. Copper said she had a lot of things at her place and I had things from my room so we will be set. 2 months till Easter and five till graduation so ready for it to be over, can't wait. Tomorrow back to school.

The next day when we got to school we had two new girls in our room. Brenda and Tracy, both were black and that was fine we had blacks in our classes. Jane and I went to dinner and when we came back to our room the floor mother was there. She asked if we would mind moving to another room, we asked why? The black girls didn't trust us and were scared. She said we could move the beds and dressers and have some girls help us move our clothes. Fine we only had five months left here. So we were moved into a larger empty room and our things put away. In the morning the staff would bring in the bookshelves and desks. We thanked everyone and went to bed. After class we went to our room and we had it all set up. The Professor of the school thanked us for not making a big mess out of it.

Nine weeks till spring break, a lot of hard work. The second week of March we were packing for home, we had four days off and then only ten weeks of school left. Mr. Copper came to our room to help with our bags. When we got to the car it was a cab, were is the car and Mrs. Copper? Just you wait and see. The cab took us to the airport and we got out. Mr. Copper said we were going to fly to Jamestown and Pete would pick us up there then home. It would only take 4 hours. Wow better than 14 hours by car. More time to spend at home. Sunday was Easter and we had a lot to do. The food and eggs went to the church on Saturday. After dinner Jane and I looked at pictures of houses that would be ready for rent in May and June. We found 3 that we liked all had 2 bedrooms, 2 baths nice kitchens and one had a sunroom that we both liked. Dad asked if we would like our rooms painted before we arrived home, Mr. Copper said he would check with the bank. All 3 were at a good price. Pete took us to the airport, we were back at school by 7:00.

Nine weeks left, we were hit with bad weather and so we stayed in most of the time. Five weeks before graduation we had to send out the invitations. I asked Jane about hers we only had 4, I was sending mom and dad. Did she want the Coppers, Yes? So we still had 4 left and her mother called while we were at dinner. She said to call her back tonight. We knew she would want tickets, she had already sent 2 to her dad and 2 for her grandparents. When she called mom said to send her 9 tickets she was bringing friends. Jane told her all tickets were gone sorry, so don't come. 2 days later she got all for tickets back with checks from all. Sorry they were going on a trip. She took her tickets to the lounge and gave them.

Chapter 29

THE LAST WEEK OF SCHOOL all we had were tests. Then the big day was here. We had our room packed up for a week. Mr. Copper was sending a truck to bring our things home. That morning we packed the truck and cars. We dressed and left for the hall. Everyone was there, so we sat in our chairs till our name was called. When my name was called mom was crying and dad yelling. As Jane crossed the stage I was crying. Soon we were on the road. So happy to be going home. Dad and Mr. Copper told us all about our house. Dad said the rooms were painted and we could move in next week. This was great, we both had jobs and would be looking at all the things the families had saved for us. Next week we will move. We had the next week off so we went to see the house Monday. All week the boys helped us move things from the barn to the house. We put everything away then made a list of things we still needed. Dishes, pots and pans, silverware and food. I'm sure we will find some odds and ends.

We had been at work for now for six weeks and were able to do the things we wanted. Worked from 8-5 then week-ends we shopped and went to the movies, Sunday was church then to the farm. Were able to pay all the bills and paid our rent every month. Then Jane's mom called. She wanted to visit for a few weeks to see our place. Jane told her we only have two bedrooms so she would have to sleep on the couch. Well then maybe for only a few days. She would be here next week-end. Jane was upset but I told her things will work out just wait and see. Told dad she was coming and dad said he would let us have a rollaway bed to use. Fine she would have a bed in the frontroom. We met her at the train at 1:45, she had five suitcases with her. Where is your car? We don't have one, it is a small town and we walk everywhere. It is only eight blocks to our house. You take two bags and we will take the rest. By the time we got home she was tired and had to rest so she laid down. Jane and I made lemonade and sat on the porch. At 5 we made dinner and woke her up, all she was saying is that the bed was like a brick. She would have to sleep in Jane's bed, Jane looked at her and told her no. We told her when she called that this was what we had and she still came. Sunday we went to church and she slept.

When we arrived home there were clothes everywhere. She started in, were do I hang all my things. Jane started to pick up all her real nice dresses and told her to pack them back up. There is no place in town to wear them. What do you do for fun? We do lunch at the café and then a movie, then back to the café for a milkshake then home. Sundays we go to church and church picnics. We go to bed at 9 because we work on Monday. That is our life. Well you need to buy a car, then you could go out more. We don't drive so there's no need for a car. Jane you need to come back to New York, there are so many young men there that you may find and marry into a nice family. Mom I love it here, not going back. This is what I want so take it or leave it. Jane looked at me and said good night I'm off to bed. I said good night and went to my room. 6:00 we were up taking showers and packing our lunches. We woke Mrs. Blake up, she told Jane she should stay home with her for a few days so they could talk alone. Jane said we get off work at 5 I will see you then. Well what am I to do in this one horse town while you are at work? I don't know, come on Sara we will be late.

We did the same thing for two days. So I told Jane at work that I was going to the farm for dinner and would be home by 9 maybe she and her mom could talk. If you need me just call. When I arrived home Mrs. Blake was crying and Jane was in her room. I knock on Jane's door and went in. What happened you both are crying and she is packing? We had a big fight and I told her to get out and not come back. I went to my room and to bed. Next day as we got home there was a car in front of the house. As we reached the porch a men came out with two suitcases. In the house Mrs. Blake was packing the overnight bag. The man came back in and said sugar are you ready? Robert I would like for you to meet my daughter and her roommate Sara. Robert said it was nice to meet us he has heard so much about us. He told Mrs. Blake they had to hurry if they were to make it to the airport on time. She looked at Jane and said they were going to Vegas to get married. Robert took the last bags out and she said, someone had to marry money so why not her. Then she left too. At dinner Jane told me that Robert was a big time lawyer in New York, Big house, a boat and lots of money. He has been after her mom for years and now he won.

Fall was here, the leaves were gold and orange. They were falling everywhere. Saturday we will have to go to the hardware store for rakes. We can play in the leaves, but when we came home from work all the leaves were gone. We called Mr. Copper and told him what happened. He laughed and said the landlord takes care of the yard so don't worry. He will make sure that the snow is removed this winter too. Just enjoy and get ready for the holidays. Dad said he would pick us up on Thanksgiving Day at 7. Mom would have breakfast ready when we got home. The house smelled great, the turkey was smelling and mom's bread was baking in the oven. We went out to the barn to help the boys. Matt and Willis still worked for mom. Peter and Paul did the sheep and we did the cows. Willis asked me if I missed all of this. I told him when I do I would just come home for a few hours. After chores we cleaned up and went to help mom. The boys came in to tell mom they would be back for milking and left. Mom made so much food you would think we were having people over. Then the back door opened and Frank and his family came in. Mom laughed, you didn't think we would forget them did you. A few minutes later the Copper' arrived we had a great time. After we cleaned up us ladies sat in the Kitchen to plan Christmas. This year it was to be at Frank and Emma's house. We all would make food to eat, Jane made great pumpkin pies so that was her job. I had the carrots and potatoes. Mom and Emma would do the rest. The boys were back then came in for pie, cake and coffee. It was time for us to leave and Willis told dad to rest they would drive us home. Did mom need anything from town? No thank you. Mom made two goodie boxes for us to take home, good thing the boys would carry them in.

I sat in front with Willis and Jane in back. Willis and I started talking about when we would ride to school in a horse and buggy. We had a good time and in 15 minutes we were home. The boys put the boxes in the kitchen and said good night. As we were putting the food away Jane asked me if it would be ok if she went out with Matt. He asked her to a movie if it was ok with me. I told her she was a big girl and can do what she wants.

She was worried because he worked for my mom, and didn't want to make trouble. I told her to go. About ten minutes later the phone rang and she ran for it, I heard her say yes Saturday night would be fine. She was on cloud 9 so happy. I was in my chair working on my Christmas gifts for the kids. I would get the other things from the store, I still liked home made things. Jane was making a sheet for her bed. She was just learning and doing a good job. She already cross stitched the pillow cases and they were great. We didn't have a TV and didn't want one. So we did a lot of sewing. We were just getting ready for bed when Jane's mother called to say Happy Thanksgiving, and to tell us what a wonderful wedding they had. Robert wanted her to come to New York for Christmas but she said she had plans. After the call we went to bed. We still had Friday to Monday off. We can go shopping and work on our gifts.

Chapter 30

*T*UESDAY AT WORK THE GUYS were talking about the war that has started overseas. They said that Pearl Harbor was attacked by Japan, the President was asking for volunteers to enlist in the Army. By now the papers were full of the war. When dad picked us up for Christmas dinner we talked about it, he told us there was now a draft to call men to join the Army. He said that Paul and Peter were still too young to go, but a lot of boys in town were already lining up at the office to enlist. Jane and Matt have be dating now for a month so he was coming to dinner. Everyone had plenty to eat and time now to get to the gifts. Frank and Emma's boys were the youngest and got theirs first. Dad gave mom a picture of a new stove and refrigerator, he told her they would be here the next day. She was so surprised. She loved them. We all loved the things we received. Matt and Jane went out to the barn to start the milking till Willis got back.

When Jane came in it looked like she was crying but put a smile on her face before mom or Mrs. Copper saw her. The boys came in for cake and coffee. They had to talk to mom and dad. Matt got his papers to join the Army and Willis was going with his, they had two weeks before they have to leave. Willis and Matt took us home. Jane cried most of the time and Matt kept telling her he was coming back and he would write. It didn't help much. Willis told me his mom was the same. His brother Tim was called up too. Mom and dad had sold most of the stock so we should be able to hire someone to work the farm.

Matt was over every night, he said we were his family now. Saturday when they were leaving the Anderson's, Coppers, Frank and Emma plus mom and dad were at the train station with them. So many boys were leaving and a lot of crying could be heard. Soon an officer said for them to board the train. So they were gone. Jane and I went home, it was a sad day. Monday at work half the men were gone and we moved the upstairs people downstairs. We had to get ready for tax season.

Days turned to weeks, weeks to months. The boys wrote lots of letters and we wrote back. There was four boys that were killed and most of the town went to the funerals. One was from our office, his family took it very hard. Everyday all you would read in the paper was about the war. A lot of families were losing sons and fathers. Every few days we worked at the church or hospital just to do our part. All the farms were sending beef, hogs, chickens and veggies to the base 50 miles from us. On September 6th, 1943 Willis walked in the office door. He was walking with a cane and had a limp. He didn't tell anyone he was hurt so we wouldn't worry. He said the war was over for him. Dad told him he would drive him home. Mrs. Anderson was so happy to have one home now she just needed Tim. Dad told us Willis wouldn't be coming back to work for mom, he had trouble standing for too long of a time. Soon we heard that Hitler was dead but left a mess in the countries he invaded. So many people were hurt or killed. Then the President was on the radio. We had just drop a bombed on Japan and the war was going to be over soon. We all thanked God for the end of the war, now please help all the men coming back to get home and get on with their lives.

The boys we sent off were coming home men, they weren't the same. Most were hurt or so skinny. Their eyes looked lost. They were coming home in groups of 5 to 15 at least once a week. Jane was so worried about Matt, no word from him in a three months. In February 1945 a soldier came in the office and asked for Jane. She started to cry, dad went to her right away. The man said he had been ordered to tell Jane that Matt was fine and will be home in two months. He was with a detail in Poland helping clean out the camps. It looked bad over there and sickening, so many bodies. He had to go see the Anderson's next to tell them Tim was dead, his body would be here in a week. Dad said he would go with him. Dad called mom and she was there when they got there. Two weeks later we had Tim's funeral. Half the men from town were dead, hurt real bad or missing. When they say War is Hell they were right.

Matt came home in June. Jane was on cloud nine. He was skinny but in good shape. He didn't want to talk about the war. That was fine with us. At first he spent a lot of time with Willis, they did the talking. Soon both guys were almost back to their old selves. The holidays were here and Matt gave Jane a ring. They would be married in June of 1946 next year. Matt had been going to night school with Willis, both were going into accounting and were working in the office at the factory in town.

Chapter 31

*W*E HAD A WEDDING TO plan. The Coppers said they would give Jane the wedding, she was like a daughter to them. Great we would work with Mrs. Copper. I asked Jane if she was going to tell her mom, sure they can come. But Mr. Copper will walk me down the aisle. We went to Jamestown to look at dresses

My word so many. We found a beautiful gown for Jane, she looked like an Angel. My dress was pale blue and Rose dress was powder blue. This would be the talk of the town. Next we looked at invitations till we found what Jane liked. Mrs. Copper talked with Jane, then wrote out the invitation it said.

Mr. & Mrs. George Copper invites you to the wedding of Miss Jane Marie Blake to Mr. Matt Spencer on June 9th 1946 at 2P.M. at the Church on the hill. Reception will follow at the Copper's home. She ordered 200 of them. I guess she was going to have the whole town there. We called Mary in Vermont to tell her. She can't come, she will be having a baby in June her third. She will send a card. We started writing the envelopes out I asked if she had her mom's address. No she would call and get it. She was on the phone a long time then came back. Mom wouldn't be coming, Robert is very sick. The doctors won't let them travel. Please send lot of pictures. They would send a check to help the Coppers.

January, February and March we were busy with taxes. In April the showers started, and we had to look for dresses. Our house started looking like a store. Matt said that their house would be done in a few weeks so we can put stuff in one of the rooms. Mr. Anderson gave Matt 100 acers and the boys are helping with the house. By the 1st of May the house was done and we started setting up her house. Three weeks before the wedding a truck arrived at the farm house. Jane's mom called Mrs. Copper and asked if they had a bedroom set and frontroom set. She said no and gave her the colors of the rooms. We told Jane that Mrs. Copper was getting them some of hers. Matt called her at work and asked her to come out after work. She was so surprised, Matt just wanted to know where she wanted everything. Soon the house was done and Matt was moving in that week-end.

When we got home she called her mom right away. She told her the colors were right and so was the style to thank Robert for her. Then mom told her that Robert was in the hospital and not doing well. She would call when something happened. We said we would pray for him, so would my family. Jane had a beautiful dress, they added some of the lace from Mrs. Copper's wedding dress. All was going very well. Jane was going to work till three days before the wedding. She would take a week off for the honeymoon. Taxes were done for the year but we still had lots to do. May 17th. Mrs. Shepherd called, Robert had passed away in his sleep. Could Jane fly up for the funeral, Jane said yes and called Matt. Mr. Copper ordered the tickets for the next day. Told them to stay a week if they wanted. The things for the wedding was all ordered things will be fine. Mrs. Shepherd ask them to stay for the reading of the will, He was a very worthy man. Everything went to his wife except for the money he left to Jane. They were so surprised and didn't want it, but mom said yes he wanted them to stock the farm. Matt said ok. She said she still wouldn't be at the wedding. It would be too soon after Robert's death, they understood.

Gifts kept coming in so we would fill Jane's car every day and take them to the farm. The week before the wedding we were off work. We did a lot of packing of Jane's things, she wanted to know if I would have a problem with the rent and bills. Told her I would be fine. The day of the wedding we girls went with Mrs. Copper to have our hair and makeup done. Mom and Rose stayed at my house till the wedding. When it was time Mr. Copper had two cars parked out front. We made it to the church, the guys were in the back. The church was full. The music started and first Rose went down she looked lovely in her blue dress, I was next. My dress was a litter darker then Roses. The music changed and Jane and Mr. Copper came down. She was a ray of sunshine. After the ceremony we did pictures, then went to the Coppers. It was a nice party and at 9:00 the couple left for the honeymoon. People started leaving so mom and I started to clean up but were stopped. There were people waiting to do it. We said good bye to everyone and left. The house was empty without Jane here, but I'll get used to it. I was starting a new time in my life.

Chapter 32

Paul and Peter were both in college. Paul was going to be a doctor and Peter a vet. Rose in high school in her last year. Then she will go to college. Where did the time go? Here it is 1948 and I'm 26 years old. I loved my job and just had dad teach me to drive. The town was growing so we had a lot of taxes to do. I loved the new stores and still walk to work and out to the farm on Sunday. Mom called me on Saturday, to say dad was on the way to the hospital, he had a heart attack. She was on her way. I left to meet her there. I was glad to see Rose was driving, mom was very upset. We found dad's room and had to wait for the doctor to see him. The doctor said dad was in a coma and didn't know if he would wake. There was nothing he could do. We called the boys and they came home. Dad passed away five days later on September 21st.1948. Dad was only 67 not that old. We laid dad to rest in the family plot by June. Mom would be placed in between both dad's. God I know mom is 65 but please leave her here with us. Uncle Ray and Uncle Roy were both gone, Aunt Carol was in a nursing home, the farms were sold. Their kids didn't want to farm. There were better jobs in the big cities.

The boys went back to school, they would both graduate in the spring. Peter was go to work for the vet in town, but Paul was going to a hospital in Chicago. He is doing his residency there. Mom and Rose were the only ones left on the farm. Mom had a man that came over every day to do the chores. Mom called me to say that she asked Aunt Kate if she would want to move to the farm. With the money from the sale of the farm she was happy in the apartment she had. She told mom she should sell the farm and move too. Mom said no she was staying put. Thanksgiving and

Christmas were both at moms. On January 29th 1949 we went to Peter's graduation he came home with us. He would be staying at the farm with mom. He started work the next week. Paul's graduation was five weeks later. On March 15th 1949 we all went. He came home for two weeks then left for Chicago.

We had a baby shower for Jane she was going to have a boy so it was fun to shop. She told Mr. Copper that when she left in six weeks she wouldn't be back. She was going to stay home with the baby. He said he wished Mrs. Copper was still here so she could see the baby. She passed away a few months before dad. So many people in my life were gone. When Jane left work we gave her a party, Mr. Copper still would go to her house on Sundays for dinner. He couldn't wait for the baby. April 25th Jane had a baby boy, we were all there for her. They named him Lawrence, Larry for short after Matt's dad. He was 20 inches long and 6.8 pounds. Looked like Matt. Mr. Copper was now a grandpa. He was happy as a lark. That Thanksgiving was at Franks and Christmas at Matt and Janes. I worked for Mr. Copper until he passed away in August of 1958. I found out that the house I was living in was in my name and all the money for the rent was in the bank in my name. He bought the home when we were in collage. He even added a lot of money to the account, and the rest of the estate to Jane. The business was sold and now I didn't have to work.

Peter and Rose came to me and we talked about mom, she was 74 now and not moving to well. Did I think we should put her in a home? Rose was in college and would be getting married in December. Peter was moving into a house in town. I told them she could move here with me. We would talk to her this weekend. Rose and I made dinner and as we ate we talked to mom. She was not happy and said she wanted to stay, he was coming soon. I explained about both dad's and she said she knew that. I told the kids I would start looking into a home for her. A week later I was called to the farm, mom had been in bed for two days and wanted to see me. Sara dad is coming for me. The farm is yours. You are the only true Crow left. The other kids were told long ago. It is up to you if you keep it or not. I sat with her and we talked about the past. We spent most of the night just talking, we laughed and cried about somethings. Then she looked at the door, She smiled and said I love you Sara, I told her I love you to mom. She smiled again and went to sleep. I called Peter and Rose they called the doctor. Three days later on February 19ᵗʰ 1959 we laid mom between both dad's. I told both of them to watch over her. Sammy and June mom is now with you show her around please.

So here I am sitting on the porch watching Wallis and Matt load up the animals. I gave them each some. Yesterday I went to the hill and said good bye to Honey. I gave all the stuff we didn't want to the shelter in town. Peter used most of the furniture for his new place. I made sure that everyone got some of the quilts mom made. She did a lot of them so I gave Jane a few. So now the house was emptied and I sold the land to a company for a factory. I have my little house in town and the kids are all set. I gave them all money from the sale. The boys will bring me the rocking chair and swing for my porch. I will be fine, I have a lot of very good friends and my family. I will start looking for a new job soon, not that I needed one just need something to do. What more would a person want?

About The Author

My name is Sharon V. Deese. I live in a small town in Florida, this is my second book. It all started when my husband John passed away. I made a bucket list there were things I wanted to do that I couldn't before. I wanted to go to Arizona to see my son, done. I wanted to go to San Diego to see the ship that my father sailed, done. I wanted to go to Mexico, done. That was the first few things.

From 27 wishes now down to two things, find someone I could love with all my heart that was done. The last thing on my list was write a book, so as I kept trying it went into the garbage. It isn't as easy as I had hoped it would be. I was working on a receiving dock when an idea started in my head so between vendors I start my first poem. It was all done by the time I left work. I don't know where the idea came from but I was writing from my heart. Always and Forever started the book. Titled Poems and short story by Sharon D. Vojtko.

I still live in a small town in Florida, and hope you will enjoy reading about a sweet little girl named Sara. Thank you and God bless everyone.

Printed in the United States
By Bookmasters